Rule

Brutal Kings (Book 1)

Via Mari

Book World Ink

Chapter 1

Chase

As we exit the limo, we are surrounded by security. The portly doorman dressed in uniform greets us as we enter the New York Prestian skyrise and head for the private elevator that will take us to our penthouse.

When the doors open into the foyer of our home, we are greeted by another man. "The condo is clear," he says to me and Sheldon, who has been placed in charge of Katarina's security.

"The Chicago boys are in the city. They're still crawling all over the Larussio estate, but the place is locked down like a fortress," one of the guards says.

"I don't want the teams getting spread too thin. Call for backup and let me know when they're in place," Sheldon says.

"Thanks, everyone," I say, knowing he'll handle any situation that may arise, and I guide Katarina through the expansive open concept condo.

Gaby is in the kitchen and wipes her hands on her apron, bustling around the counter to pull Katarina into her arms and then me. "Land sakes! The boys weren't telling me anything. I didn't even know you were safe until just a few moments ago. Shame on you for keeping me in the dark," Gaby says, smacking me playfully on the arm.

The woman who has been like a surrogate mother to me and has maintained my homes for the last seven years was worried. "Sorry, Gaby, they had to be extra careful. We were supposed to be on our way to Italy and wanted anyone trying to find us to believe that was still the plan," I say.

"You know I worry," Gaby says, sashaying her round figure to the counter to pour each of us a cup of coffee.

"No need, Gaby. It's being sorted," I say, helping Katarina settle onto the barstool.

"Hmm! Says you! Sit. I figured if your security team wanted me here that you were up to no good. I have some blueberry mix made, and it won't take long to make you both some pancakes," Gaby says, opening the refrigerator to pull out a ceramic bowl covered in saran wrap while we drink our coffee.

She bustles about the kitchen, getting our breakfast prepared, and places the blueberry pancakes on the table. The aroma wafts through the air, and Katarina's face pales.

"You okay, Baby?" I ask.

"My stomach still isn't quite right," she says quietly.

Gaby takes a close look at her. "Rough night?" she says to Katarina and gives me a scowl.

Katarina smiles. "It's not his fault. We were celebrating Jenny's exoneration, and I had way too much to drink last night. My head is pounding. Hopefully, the Ibuprofen kicks in soon," Katarina says.

"I know just the cure, Sweetie," Gaby says, pulling out a can of tomato juice, a lemon, hot sauce, and going to the bar to grab a bottle of vodka. "The best thing in the world for a hangover is a

Bloody Mary," Gaby declares as she begins whipping her concoction together.

"Gaby, she has a lot of work to do in order to prepare for an important meeting this afternoon," I admonish.

She narrows her eyes into slits at me. "And if she drinks this, her headache will be gone. She's dehydrated, needs some salt, a bit of spice, the vitamins in the tomato juice, and just a little hair of the dog. It's not strong, and she'll be better in no time," Gaby says, placing her concoction emphatically in front of Katarina and handing her a straw.

"I've never had a Bloody Mary, but I'm willing to try anything at this point," Katarina says, initially sipping the drink tentatively and then taking large pulls from the straw until she has finished it in entirety.

"That was really good! I'm sure I feel at least a little better," Katarina says laughing, handing Gaby her empty glass.

Gaby raises her eyebrows in triumph. "Of course you do, child. Now let's make you one without the vodka. The sodium and other nutrients you lost last night will be replaced shortly enough," she says, bustling to the counter to blend the drink.

I watch on with amusement as another glass is placed in front of Katarina and she chugs that one, too.

"It's been in my family for generations. You'll be good as new in no time, just like magic. Now you need to eat, loads of carbs and real butter to soak up that alcohol," Gaby says, placing the stack of pancakes in front of us once again and slathering Katerina's with Irish cream butter.

Katarina grins at me mischievously and takes a bite and then another. I want to do something utterly obscene with that mouth of hers, but my phone begins to vibrate with message after message, turning my attention to it. I excuse myself from their conversation, hit my attorney's number and listen to him for a few brief moments.

"Have it delivered to me at our condo in the city ASAP. I'll review it and be in touch," I say, hanging up and looking into the questioning sea-blue eyes of my wife.

"What was that all about?" Katarina says, passing me her plate with one untouched pancake heavily laden with butter.

I ignore her question and push her plate back toward her, gesturing for her to eat while Gaby still has her back turned. "So full," she whispers, rubbing her belly by way of explanation.

I smirk and take pity on her, brushing the uneaten pancake onto my plate, just before Gaby turns back to Katarina. "Good, you've cleaned your plate. You'll feel better in no time," she says, nodding with confidence.

My baby's curiosity is not to be deterred though. "What was your conversation about?" Katarina asks as Gaby walks back into the kitchen with our plates.

"It was our attorney. Carlos updated his will and living power of attorney documents a while back, naming the two of us co-executors of the Larussio estate, with detailed instructions on how he wants his empire to be handled."

Her brow furrows with concern for her father.

"You heard me tell our attorney the swelling in his brain is leveling off. There's every indication he'll get through this, but until he does, he safeguarded his empire to ensure the legacy he wants for his family comes to life. He named you and one of your cousins, Giovanni Larussio, as the sole beneficiaries if both parents are deceased, with a wealth of contingencies that need to be fulfilled. We can review it once we receive the details."

"If he's going to pull through, why would he do that now?" Katarina asks.

"He drew it up before the accident. He's not well enough yet to take the reins, and so this document has taken effect per his time stipulations. Carlos trusts you will honor his wishes while he's unable to handle the business himself, and knows I won't let anyone stand in your way."

"I have absolutely no experience with anything like this. The family barely knows me, and there are about a million other reasons, including this headache from hell, that leave me completely incompetent to deal with this," Katarina says, but I cut her off gently, taking her hand in mine.

"You will do fine," I say as I stand.

"I'm still processing," Katarina says, her eyes gliding over my body, the path of her eyes heating my skin as it settles on my cock, which hardens with the desire of her gaze.

I clear my throat and smirk as I lean over and kiss the tip of her nose, taking in the sparkling blue eyes and heated cheeks. She knows I've caught her admiring the view, and I love how her flushed cheeks give her need away. "I'm having the documents delivered shortly. That's the conversation you overheard," I say, taking a drink of my coffee.

She shakes her head, and her long auburn curls sway with the movement. "If they are the ones that hurt my parents, I will not stop until they pay. They are stupid if they'd don't think that I have what it takes to go up against that family."

My jaw tightens at the very thought of her in harm's way. "Katarina, your dad will pull through this. You are a Larussio and will rise to the challenge, but you should rest before we prepare for your meeting with your uncle and Gio later," I say, pushing a wayward strand of hair behind her ear.

She nods and nuzzles into my chest as I pick her up and carry her to our room, settling her into the king-size bed to undress her and caress her with my tongue until she is sated and sleepy. I intend to leave her in our bed alone, but her arms wrap around my neck, and I curl her into my arms as she drifts to sleep.

I look down at my wife, her long auburn hair splayed across her back and watch the gentle rise and fall of her chest for the next half an hour as she rests, carefully slipping out of bed so as not to wake her once she falls into a deep slumber. There is much to do today to ensure the safety of my spirited young wife.

Chapter 2

Gio

I stare out to the blue-green sea crashing against the Amalfi Coast so far below. This view from my home office, which usually settles my agitation, does nothing to calm me today.

I reread the message from my great-uncle requesting me to travel to the United States to meet my cousin Katarina Meilers Larussio Prestian, the daughter of my favorite uncle, Carlos Larussio. My jaw shifts with annoyance. The family members who have met my cousin seem to love her, but I haven't seen a paternity test or any evidence that would positively conclude she is a Larussio, and until Uncle Carlos is well enough to have visitors or speak on the phone, there's no reason to journey that far.

I send my great-uncle an email letting him know that I have no interest in flying halfway across the globe to talk business, knowing he wants me on the plane in less than two hours. A message from our security team arrives, alerting me that the package my attorney needs me to review has arrived.

I stride down the stairs toward the great room, but Victor, the estate butler, is already at the door accepting it as I walk up behind him. He hands it to me while thanking the delivery driver, and I head back to my study to read its contents. I close the heavy mahogany door to my office, slide into the leather executive chair, and open the sealed envelope.

My chest tightens when I see that it is Uncle Carlos Larussio's living will. If his attorney is sending me this, his health must be deteriorating. Dammit! I should have been there when he first got in the accident, and would have been if it hadn't been for those damn negotiations. If that deal had gone south, it would have meant the loss of thousands of jobs in the area. I know Carlos would have wanted me to stay and seal the deal. If it hadn't been for that, I would have been on the first plane over, hospital rules and security clearance be damned. This makes no sense at all. I've talked to Don Prestian, my uncle's best friend, almost every day and have had every indication that he is getting better but still is not well enough to receive visitors or I would have been to see him already.

I read the first two pages and already have questions, the third through the fifth are complex and full of stipulations to ensure the vast Larussio resort he wants to create in the United States moves ahead swiftly. I'm only halfway through the document when a call comes in from my great-uncle.

"Giovanni, Carlos must be in a bad way. It's been too long since we've spoken. I'm going to America, with or without you," he says.

Even though I've had no indication his health is declining, I'm holding his living will in my hand, and that can't be good. "When do we leave?" I say, changing my mind, knowing that I can take care of my other commitments in the air.

"The Prestian Corporation has a jet at the airport right now refueling from an overseas trip and will be leaving for the States soon. I talked with Don Prestian, and his son is making arrangements for us to be on that flight," my great-uncle says.

"Why his plane when ours is in the private hangar?" I ask.

"I'll fill you in on the way over," he says.

"I'll be ready. Do we have any details about Carlos?" I ask.

"We don't know much, Giovanni. It's too early. They put him in a coma to let the swelling in his brain subside, and they've brought him out of it, but only time will tell."

"There's never been any love lost between you two. Why travel halfway around the world to see him?"

"I'm also meeting with my great-niece Katarina and her husband. I want you to come with me and meet your cousin," my great-uncle says.

"You mentioned that before. What are you expecting to learn that we don't already know?" I ask about this alleged daughter of Carlos who is currently listed as a beneficiary in Carlos's living will along with myself.

"I asked you to come with me because something's not right. Carlos may not have been acting of sound mind even before he was in the accident," he says.

Now it's coming together. Great-uncle has somehow received a copy of Carlos's will and knows he has not been named in it, not one mention at all, as though he doesn't exist. I smile to myself. Of course, in my great-uncle's mind, that would be completely insane.

"We didn't originally think his accident had anything to do with us, but it may be the Chicago Mafia, and if it is, they're not going to stop with Carlos and his family in New York. You can be damned sure that our entire family will be in jeopardy," my great-uncle says.

I'm convinced this trip is more about the will than anything, but at least now I understand why we're taking a Prestian jet. He's concerned about the Chicago Family. We've got a long trip ahead of us and plenty of time to talk, so I let it go. "Let's continue our discussion in the air. I have a few things that require my attention before we leave. I'll meet you at the airport," I say, listening a few more minutes before we both disconnect.

"I'll have your bags prepared shortly," Victor says, having heard my conversation while walking through the dining room. I nod and mouth my thanks while connecting to my attorney.

He answers after a few rings. "I need a favor, and this can't go through the family security. Can you get me an in-depth background on Katarina Meilers Larussio Prestian?" I ask.

"I thought you might want that once you read the documents. I've already sent through the request," Thomas says.

"Excellent. Hopefully, the jet we're taking back is wired," I say, still annoyed we're using the Prestian Corp jet to America and not one of our own.

"I'll get you the information as soon as it arrives," Thomas says.

"One last thing, have you spoken to my great-uncle about the content of the documents you sent over this morning?" I ask.

"He wasn't named. I wouldn't have any reason to talk to him. Why do you ask?" Thomas says.

"I would bet a good deal that he already knows exactly what those documents contain. I'm more than curious how he got his hands on the information," I say.

"You can be assured the information didn't come from this office. I was contacted directly by Carlos's attorney, and it was delivered to me personally with a copy for you. I would presume he contacted Katarina's attorney and that by now she has a copy, too."

"I'll look into it a little bit later. Thanks again," I say, disconnecting and heading to my suite to get showered and dressed for the trip.

* * *

When I return downstairs, my bags and briefcase are already by the door. "The car will be around momentarily. Your passport and electronics are in the side pocket of your brief," Victor says as the driver pulls up in a sleek black Lincoln and steps out of the car to open my door. I wave him away and climb into the back.

The driver navigates the traffic with a security car in front of and behind us all the way to the airstrip. As he pulls up to the private entrance of the airport, my uncle is waiting, along with his entire entourage. My jaw shifts with frustration that our family has such a need for security, seemingly always on someone's list for revenge. This is what happens when your family has a history like ours, revered and respected by some, but hated by many.

He pulls me close and kisses each cheek, and regret for thinking of him so poorly surfaces. My great-uncle would do anything for anyone in our family. He took me in at an early age when my parents were killed. While not supportive of me branching out and going into business on my own, he did not stop me when I made it clear that's what I wanted to do, although he could have done precisely that.

"How are you?" I ask, realizing he looks wearier than I've seen before.

"I'm well, Giovanni. Just a little tired, but I have to admit, I'm looking forward to resting on the way over."

"Good. Let's hope this thing we're flying in is comfortable," I say, still rankling somewhat at not taking my own jet. The Larussio jets are the newest and top of the line, but as we walk out to the tarmac, a powerful, sleek plane is pulling up to the ramp in front of us. I smirk to myself looking at the almost identical model of my own Gulfstream, only in white with a substantial black Prestian Corp emblem on the tail. A couple of our security guards have already boarded to clear the plane while the others escort us across the tarmac and onto the plane.

The pilot introduces himself and his copilot, and after a few moments of weather talk, we are escorted into the main cabin. Whoever designed the interior was talented. The windows are long and oval, maximizing the natural midmorning light streaming in. The leather couch is situated underneath the windows and then curves into the cabin, allowing extra seating around a large fireplace with a television monitor over the mantle. The sleek black bar in the corner is a nice touch. I walk through the main cabin, opening the door to the impressively decorated master bedroom.

The utilization of space is impressive, with drawers underneath the queen-size bed, and television monitor over the fireplace in this room too, along with a large puffy chair with a crocheted afghan tossed over it, making the room look lived-in. I peek into the bathroom and nod, taking in the dual showerheads and sleek corner design that provides more usable space throughout. I walk back out into the main cabin and tell the security team they can put my uncle's things in the bedroom.

He looks like he should rest, and as soon as we take off, my great-uncle lets me know he's off to do just that. I settle into the large chair in the main cabin, taking out the documents from my briefcase. I've barely start to read when the door opens and a short-skirted leggy blonde with a couple too many buttons undone on her blouse saunters in, giving me a clear view of excellent cleavage.

I half-smile, hoping my disdain isn't apparent as she sashays over. You can see them coming from a mile away, every damn one of them. They should have a tattoo that says, Will fuck if you are rich.

"I didn't get a chance to introduce myself when you boarded. We were preparing the security quarters and galley for the return trip," the blonde says, holding out her hand to me. "I'm Brigett, and will be servicing you during the flight," she says, winking at me.

I smirk. She didn't need the wink—I didn't miss the innuendo. "Well, Brigett, I'll most definitely let you know if I require service," I say as the door opens again, and this time I find myself staring at a dark-haired beauty with deep-set brown eyes with golden flecks that seem to flash as she watches the exchange. She pushes a wisp of her waist-long hair out of her eyes, and her naturally-colored plump red lips tighten with disdain.

"Mr. Larussio, I was just going to stop in and introduce myself. My name is Serena, and if you need anything during your flight, the button on the bottom of the remote will alert us," she says, spinning before I've even had a chance to finish looking at her.

The blonde rolls her eyes and winks like we have a shared secret, and I scowl at her in return. Serena walks toward the door, and my eyes are mesmerized by the inward curve of her waist and the outer curve of her ass and hips. My dick enlarges, pushing uncomfortably against my zipper, letting me know he's right there with me as she walks out of the door.

"Now, where were we?" the blonde bombshell says, leaning over to give me another look at her tits.

"I think you were done, and I was about to read the document in my hands," I say, looking at her painted face, bleached hair, and black-mascara-framed eyes blinking up at me.

She pretends to pout, but when that doesn't work she shrugs and turns, walking toward the security room. I send a text to my security team to keep her busy and out of my way.

My thoughts turn toward the dark-eyed sultry beauty, the one with the body that makes my cock throb. I could use a drink, and smile to myself as I hit the button on the bottom of the remote.

Chapter 3

Serena

My heart is clamoring in my chest as I slip into the galley quarters behind the flight crew. This man, Giovanni Larussio, I would recognize him anywhere. Little did I know when I agreed to this trip that I would be flying with that vile man! Brigett not only doesn't seem to care what type of people she spends time with, but doesn't waste a minute cozying up to the rich and elite men we are paid to provide attendant service to. The man barely had time to settle in before she pounced, but it certainly didn't look like the womanizer minded having her chest in his face.

The same thing, every trip we make together. As soon as the captain and copilot are locked into the cockpit, she assumes that she can do as she pleases. I know I should say something, put a stop to it, but the simple truth is that if she's keeping our flight guests entertained, they will not bother me, and that suits me just fine.

They are not all like that, coming onto the help, but so many are, and the dread that I will lose my job if I displease someone is always on my mind. Brigett must have undone the other buttons of her blouse after she left the flight crew and me. I can only hope they keep each other company the entire flight back and stay out of my hair.

I should have turned down the last-minute request to be part of the service crew for a flight from Italy to America, but the pay was too good to pass up. If I had known Giovanni would be on this plane, no amount of money would have made me accept this trip. I pick up a paperback novel, flipping to my bookmarked page, and have just settled in to read when the button above the galley door flashes and beeps, alerting me that our guest needs something in the main cabin. Surely Brigett could have taken care of the man's needs!

I open the door, and Mr. Larussio is looking down intently, reading through a pamphlet of papers. When he looks up, his deep brown eyes hold mine for a few fleeting moments, but I will myself to cut the connection and look away. When I glance back at him, he is smiling, watching me with an odd intensity that sends a small shiver down the length of my spine.

Giovanni Larussio, Mafioso, is known to everyone, on all of the magazines touted as one of the world's wealthiest and most eligible bachelors, with a different long-legged model on his arm every few days. He is dressed in a luxurious black suit with a crisp white shirt that seems even more pronounced against his olive skin, which has been bronzed by the sun. His dark black hair, brown eyes, and gold neck jewelry look like he could have just stepped off a luxury yacht. I briefly wonder what he would look like in swim trunks, but will myself not to look down because I know who he really is under all the generous contributions he makes, and what he and his family are really capable of.

"I was wondering if perhaps I could get a drink," Giovanni says, bringing my wandering mind back to the present.

"Yes, absolutely. Where did Brigett go?" I ask, wondering why she isn't still with him.

"I think the security team is keeping her busy," Mr. Larussio says, smiling widely at me, showing a perfect set of white teeth.

"That's too bad. I thought Brigett could service your needs for the rest of the trip," I say, heading around the backside of the bar in the corner. I bite my lip, unsure what has come over me. Arrogant or not, this man is a guest of Chase Prestian, one of the wealthiest men in the world and who employs my company to ensure he and those that travel in his planes are comfortable, and I can ill afford to lose my job.

I am about to apologize, but he raises his eyebrows and smirks at me. "I'm not sure providing a drink was exactly what your friend had in mind when she offered to service my needs," Giovanni says, and my cheeks flush. Well, the man's definitely got her number.

"What would you like to drink?" I ask, keeping my eyes lowered as I shuffle glasses around the bar.

"Let's try something different than wine. Scotch will do," Giovanni says, and that husky velvety voice makes my center clench.

"Dalmore okay?" I ask, knowing how outrageously expensive it is and that it's kept onboard for Brian Carrington when he travels in the Prestian Corp plane. It is his favorite, and Chase likes to make sure his best friend is comfortable when he flies with him.

"Excellent choice, actually," Giovanni says as I begin to pour. I walk toward him and can feel my cheeks heat and skin tingle as his eyes take in every inch of my body.

I extend my hand to give him the drink, and his fingers curl around my own as he takes it from me, just a brief second, but the heat of his touch causes my body to thrum. I can feel myself blush deeply and pull my hand quickly away.

"Would you like to join me?" Giovanni asks, his dark eyes waiting for an answer as I watch, mesmerized by his lips parting to taste his drink.

"Thank you, but no. I'm on duty and need to get things ready for when your uncle wakes from his nap," I say, spinning and heading toward the door, all the while still feeling the intensity of his gaze on my body.

Only after I close the door and am safe in the small service area does my heart rate begin to slow after having come so close to one of the men I hate and the genuine physical effect he has had on me. I busy myself preparing a light tray of Pane e Olio, tasty bread with olive oil to dip it in, and Pane e Pomodoro, another crusted bread rubbed with tomato and seasoned lightly, pairing it with Maritozzo, a slightly oval-shaped bread split open and filled with homemade cream for those with a sweeter preference. I cover the treats for serving later and hit the button on my phone that will connect me with Nonna.

Her voice comes on the line, and although she sounds a little tired, it doesn't seem weak. I listen to her tell me about her day and my heart aches at the thought that one day soon I may lose her, but I try to push those thoughts away, attempting to cherish each day that I have with her. We usually have much more time together between flights, and this jet was supposed to go back to the States with just the captain and copilot. At the last minute, passengers were added and they needed a crew.

My company, who provides attendant services to the private jet industry, had to scramble to ensure flight attendants were available. The extra bonus for no notice and double the pay for this flight will help with anything necessary to keep Nonna comfortable, so when asked to make the trip, it was not even a choice.

Nonna loves to hear about the exotic places that we fly to, and I have spent countless hours by her bedside, and on the phone, enlightening her with the details about each and every exotic destination that I have traveled to. I leave out the fact that I have not experienced them once myself, and that instead I have Googled the places in flight or from a hotel room to give her such vast descriptions.

This time, I also leave out the fact that I am on board with the well-known Larussio family, knowing she would be absolutely terrified for my safety. Nonna begins to tire after a short time and I wish I could be there to cover her as she drifts to sleep, and I disconnect.

Brigett must have found someone to keep her company and hasn't yet returned, which is more than fine by me. I slip off my shoes and curl up in a cozy chair and have just finished the first chapter of my novel when the flashing lights and beep alert me that someone in the main cabin needs something.

Seriously! I shake my head in disgust just knowing that Giovanni Larussio is going to be one of those high maintenance, arrogant men that I have come to loathe. I don't know why I am surprised in the least. I expected it from the very time recognition set in, but I thought Brigett would be more than delighted to keep him company, just like every other rich man that we travel with.

If he wants another drink and started in the morning, he's probably one of those heavy drinkers. We get them sometimes. That's not entirely fair, given the time difference in Italy, and I know it, but still. I sigh deeply, putting my heels back on, running a hand down my skirt to smooth it before opening the door to the main cabin. He's at the bar in the corner, with paperwork spread out all over the top of it, his cell phone is out, and he's typing something on his laptop. His black suit coat is now draped over the reading chair he was in the last time I was in the room.

I have a hard time not staring at his broad shoulders and tapered waist from behind. His lean and taught muscles are clearly visible under his crisp white dress shirt that has been rolled up to his elbows, displaying corded forearms. I glance up, realizing he's watching me scrutinizing him from the mirror behind the bar. My cheeks heat with embarrassment at being caught. Damn him for being so . . . hot!

He's smirking, and now I know what that American saying about wanting the floor to open up and swallow you is all about. "Did you need something, Mr. Larussio? Where is Brigett? I would have thought she would have returned and been attending to your needs," I say, trying my best to avoid the dark hooded eyes still holding mine intently through the reflection in the mirror.

"My father has just awakened and will join me shortly. Would you be able to bring a light meal out for him?" Giovanni asks.

"Of course. I have prepared Pane e Olio, Pane e Pomodoro, and Maritozzo. Is that okay?" I ask.

"Perfezionare, I'll let the vino breathe while you're gone," Giovanni says, and I don't know why, but the fact that he's so pleased with what I've prepared makes me tingle inside.

I head to the service area and gather the tray, carry it back to the main cabin, and place it on the bar in front of him. "I hope you and your father will enjoy the merenda."

"Which company do you work for?" Giovanni asks, suddenly swiveling on his stool to face me.

I stand before him and feel the blood drain from my face. I thought he was pleased, but if he's caught onto my contempt, that is most definitely not good. My pulse begins to race through my veins because he can ensure with one call that my job is over. It will then be impossible to find work making the kind of money I need.

"Serena, I asked you a question, no?" Giovanni asks, and I start at the sound of his voice.

"I'm sorry, it was not my intention to displease you, Mr. Larussio," I say.

He scowls slightly, and his jaw tightens while his eyes fixate on my own. "You think you displeased me? Serena, what are you apologizing for, Bella Donna?" Giovanni asks, his deep eyes holding mine captive.

"I was disrespectful. It's just that Brigett usually stays close to our special patrons," I say, knowing that he holds both Nonna's and my own life in his hands.

His fingers snake under my hair, grasping my nape, and he pulls me closer causing my pulse to race. "You weren't respectful in the way I am accustomed to, but you weren't disrespectful. What are you scared of?" Giovanni asks, whispering in my ear.

My pussy clenches with need, and I can only hope he can't see the erectness of my nipples, but his gaze lowers, and his eyes darken with desire.

"I know who you are, who your family is, but I desperately need my job," I say, and tense as his hand snakes around my waist, pulling me even closer to him.

"Take a seat, Serena, and for the record, the name is Gio," he says, patting the barstool next to him.

Chapter 4

Katarina

I am freshly showered and wrapped in a luxurious body towel, looking out over the vast city of New York, taking in the bright lush green treetops that form the sprawling rectangle that is Central Park, when Chase walks back into the bedroom.

He's freshly showered and dressed, looking like he just stepped out of an executive conference with his dark suit, sparkling cuff links, and tie. "Sleep well, Baby?" he asks.

"Mmm. So good. I love the way you tuck me in," I say, blushing at the memory of being restrained with my silver bracelets while he made me come so hard, capturing every bit of energy left before I fell asleep.

Chase smirks at me and his green eyes dance with mischief. "I'm always happy to help with that. Come and sit with me," Chase says, taking a seat in the large armchair, opening his arms, and pulling me down to settle into his lap as I reach him. "I know we went over a lot, but I've been reviewing another document our attorney just sent over. It's pretty complicated and outlines explicitly what he wants, right down to the finest detail. It's basically a roadmap of how his empire will run if he is incapacitated, and any deviation from that requires loops of law and legal procedure that would get held up in court for years. Katarina, your father is a genius. What do you know about your cousin Giovanni Larussio?"

"Not much really. Giovanni was traveling when everything went down with Mom and at the time of our wedding. Dad's never mentioned him to me," I say.

"I didn't think your father was close with any of the Larussios, but he's apparently left him in charge of the operational side of the Vegas Empire," Chase says.

"That doesn't make any sense. According to Dad, none of the family wants anything to do with the Vegas deal," I say.

"I'm having a background check run on him, but for now, you're in charge of ensuring the facility is brought up to the specifications laid out under Torzial Consulting and the customer experience. However, once it's up, he will be in charge of putting the day-to-day operations in place to support that vision, with both of you owning fifty-fifty, and your father has put me in charge of seeing that it's done as he intends. You'll want to read it yourself," Chase says.

While I have struggled in the past giving him control, that is not the case now. He wants me to read through it, but I know without a doubt that he already has and a plan is already in place that will ensure our family's safety and sustainability long term. I lean forward and kiss his lips. "Pretty sure you can just give me the highlights, but I just don't get that Dad's never mentioned Giovanni once."

He pulls me harder into his lap, his hands around my hips, grinding my center into his hardened length. "I've asked our attorney to join us when we meet with your father's uncle and Giovanni. They should be arriving shortly. One of our jets was still over in Italy, and I made arrangements with my dad for them to use that for the trip over," Chase says, sliding me against his erection.

"Time to meet the scary great-uncle, I guess. What else did you do while I was sleeping, blissfully unaware of all the drama while you were taking care of the world?" I ask, smiling.

"He put you in charge because he knows you're quite capable, but he's also provided every support possible to ensure you are successful in fulfilling his dream for the family in the future. No one, not even his brother, uncles, or anyone can interfere with his plans for the Vegas build, not even Giovanni Larussio. The outline you created under Torzial Consulting needs to be followed to the letter. Our attorneys have been poring over this since they received the document from your father's attorney's office. Carlos made sure your family didn't have a leg to stand on if they opposed you," Chase says, pulling me closer and pushing a strand of wayward hair out of my eyes before kissing my lips gently.

I swallow.

"This doesn't mean that your dad won't pull through," Chase says, caressing my cheek, his deep green eyes watching intently.

I nod, trying desperately not to think of my father near his deathbed but instead on his way to recovery, but my great-uncle in New York City means that he will be too close to those I love. I need to calm myself before our meeting, because at this very moment I want to do that man great harm. I also know that I need to finesse the bastard to protect my parents and the legacy my father has worked toward for over twenty years.

I feel the heat of Chase's gaze and look up into the deep green eyes watching me process this information. "Katarina, you are the only daughter of the man in charge of the New York City Mafia. While he wants a different life for his family in the future, it doesn't change the fact that his family is still supported by much of the legacy funds. They'll need to be assured his plan will sustain them and their families in the future, or all of your relatives will side with your great-uncle."

The responsibility of ensuring our family's future is on my shoulders. My father entrusted me with this duty, and while I can't deny fear of the unknown, a surge of pride fills me that he trusted me enough to leave this job to me. "I can do this and will do this," I say as Chase pushes the auburn hair that has fallen over my eyes out of my face.

"You were formidable with Vicenti, and I don't expect anything different with your great-uncle, but they could have been the ones that attempted to take your father out with a semi-truck, and I'm not going to be able to sit idly by without getting involved. You need to know now that it's not going to happen, Baby," Chase says, lifting my chin so that I am caught by the emotion swirling in his deep green eyes.

I nod, knowing this is hard for my husband, who is overly enthusiastic when it comes to keeping me safeguarded, and while there was a time his need for control to do that rankled, it no longer does. I take his face in my hands and kiss his lips gently. "That's good because I never want to do anything without you," I say, wondering how I could love this man any more.

I glance at my favorite leggings and socks. These are me, my clothes of choice, what I am comfortable in, but I will be going head-to-head with my great-uncle, who wants to prove my father was incapacitated when he put me in charge. My great-uncle wants to discredit Carlos, to ruin my father's legacy, and I will not allow it! "I need a totally different look, new clothes. My great-uncle needs to know that he's dealing with a Larussio, not the timid little Meilers girl," I say.

Chase is watching me intently, his eyes taking it all in, and nods his approval. "That's my girl. I can see the passion in your eyes. Is that how you felt when you went against Vicenti," he asks, caressing my cheek.

I nod, but when I went to visit the head of the South American Cartel, I was fueled by fear that I would never see Chase outside of prison bars. "It wasn't much of a decision. Meeting Vicenti was the only way to get you freed and returned to me. I would have done anything, and now I need to do the same for my dad and the future he wants for our family. I need different clothes, undergarments, thigh-highs, lacy little camis, power suits, and heels, four-inch fuck-me heels by the best designers in the business to play this role!" I say.

His eyes darken. "I hated the look in Vicenti's eyes when you crossed your bare legs in that little thing you called a skirt, and damn, those high heels were hot. I could feel the way he wanted you through the video on my attorney's phone," Chase says.

I lean over and kiss his lips gently. "I did what was needed to get you home."

"As much as I love you submissive, allowing me to care for all of your needs, I saw the satisfaction in your eyes when you freed me. You rose up, fought for what you wanted, and I couldn't have been more proud, aside from the fact that you looked hot and formidable."

"Somehow you always know exactly how to make me feel better," I say.

He wraps his arms around me. "The time you told me that you didn't think about what you were doing? You didn't have to, it's instinctual; it's in your blood, Katarina. You are a Larussio, the mafia boss's daughter, put in charge of the family and you will earn their trust."

"I sure hope so! It's a little unnerving," I say.

"My cock gets hard just thinking about you the way you looked that day. In fact, I kept the text you sent to Sheldon asking him to get you specific clothes before you went to see Vicenti. I had our shopper purchase some clothes while we were on our way home from LA. Go look," Chase says, gesturing toward the closet.

When will Chase ever not anticipate my needs before I know them myself? I scoot out of the chair we're in and walk into the closet, gasping audibly. There are so many things. "Chase, you shouldn't have spent so much of your money," I say, looking back to him.

He narrows his eyes at me. "Baby, it's our money, and the next time you forget that, I'll put you over my knee and you won't be able to sit down for a week," Chase says, the flash of emotion in his deep hazel green eyes letting me know that he would happily do just that.

My entire body thrums with the dynamic we share. Chase is entirely dominant, needing to take care of me, both in and out of the bedroom, and always looking out for my best interests. He guides me through the most significant challenges in life while providing me with the most erotic sexual journey I have ever experienced.

"There will be someone arriving to do your hair and makeup shortly. In the meantime, I think you should put on the black-and-red panty-and-bra set you have and then try on a few outfits," Chase says, settling back into the chair and toeing off his shoes.

"And you're just going to sit there and watch while I do?" I ask.

His eyes darken with desire. "I'm going to inspect every bit of lacy material you put on that impressive little body of yours while you decide what you want to wear for this meeting," Chase says, smiling widely.

"You're seriously going to watch me try on all of these clothes?" I ask, watching his deep green eyes focused on mine dilate with desire.

"Of course, that's why I purchased so many," Chase says, smirking darkly.

That brings a smile to my lips. Game on! I open my dresser and select the skimpiest black thong in my collection, slowly sliding it up my legs and around my hips before the red bow settles to rest on the top of my mound.

He leans back in his chair to watch, and my center tightens at the site of the bulge underneath his dress pants. "A reverse striptease. I shouldn't like this as much as I do. Keep going," Chase says.

Chapter 5

Chase

Katarina selects a black demi bra with red lace to pair with her thong, placing her hands on her breasts, caressing them before closing the clasp. My cock strains with desire, pushing against my dress pants and visibly tenting the material.

She opens one after another of the garment bags holding suits I've had purchased for her, and then she gasps. "Chase, this is exactly the one. It reminds me of Vegas, it's absolutely perfect," Katarina says, holding up a short black skirt with a black jacket adorned with a thin red pocket and a bit of lace. She pulls them from the dress bag and takes them off the hangers, eager to try them on.

"I think you'll find a couple blouses and camis in the bag to the right," I say, gesturing with my hand to the end of the closet.

There must be at least ten different blouses and ten different silky and lacy tanks hanging in her closet, but a quick swipe through them brings her to the exact one she's looking for: a bright white camisole with gorgeous red lace decorating its edges. She takes it from its hanger and slides it over her head, tucking it into the skirt and zipping it in the back. She spins around in front of the mirror, and I can tell she's feeling much more confident.

"Thank you so much. The ensemble couldn't be more perfect," Katarina says.

"Pretty sure my baby needs an incredibly sexy and powerful set of heels to go with the outfit she'll wear walking into the Italian Mafia world. You'll find a selection to choose from in the boxes to the right of the closet," I say, watching her ass as she bends over to pick up the boxes while I shift to relieve my cock from the restraints of the zipper it's growing against.

She opens the first two boxes and appears delighted with the choices, but I can tell they are not the ones. "They are beautiful, and I know exactly which of my outfits I can wear each of them with," Katarina says, and I watch with amusement as she opens the third box, hoping they will be just what she is looking for.

The look on her face before she even says a word tells me the shopper understood precisely what I described and selected well. "Chase, they're perfect, like someone knew exactly what I would be looking for and hand-picked it for me. Oh, my God, I can't believe how perfect they are with this outfit," Katarina says, admiring the four-inch Jimmy Choos. She slips into the black patent leather with a red platform and stick-heel, and while she admires the shoes in the full-length mirror, I appreciate the view. The height of the pumps extends her calves and thighs, which are only covered by the sleek Aruban moisturizer she uses that leaves them smooth and glossy.

She spins in front of the mirror, and my cock throbs hard at the same time my chest tightens with the thought of her going face-to-face with these people, and it is an internal struggle not to keep her far away from this situation, protected and safe.

"Chase, it's absolutely perfect," Katarina says.

"Almost. Put your jacket on and let's see how it looks together," I say, walking toward her to take it from the hanger and hand it to her.

She slides on the jacket and spins for me. "What do you think?" she asks.

"I think you look like a very hot mafia boss's daughter," I say huskily.

"You like?" Katarina asks, spinning again.

"It's more important that you like it and that you feel confident wearing it. I personally like you in no clothes," I say, pulling my wife into my arms and capturing her sweet tasting lips. "Now finish getting ready before I can't be held responsible for your tardiness," I say, smacking her playfully on the ass before heading downstairs and leaving her to finish dressing.

I saw that flicker of heat, the look in those mesmerizing blue eyes of hers, letting me know she's already contemplating and planning her meeting with her great-uncle, even before she knows all the details.

My mind drifts to the time she forced one of my security members to take her to Brazil so she could get him to help me out of a false accusation, and my jaw tightens so hard it pulls me back to the task at hand. All the way across the globe, facing one of the most notorious South American crime bosses like she was going for an afternoon visit. She will do whatever it takes for those she loves, and I've seen it time and time again, and it furthers my resolve to be three steps ahead of my adventurous little wife.

I know Katarina told me that she needs my help, exactly what she thinks I want to hear, but I also know that if there is any danger for me or her parents, she will try to take matters into her own hands. If she thinks she's going up against the goddamn Italian Family on her own, my wife is wrong, and may just end up learning that the hard way with a trip across my lap.

The thought of her bare ass bent over my lap causes my cock to harden again. I adjust myself before easing into one of the dining room chairs and pour a cup of coffee from the carafe. I wonder if the need to protect, the desire and lust I feel for her will always be this primal, hot, molten, and intense.

I pull myself away from my erotic thoughts and open the documents that have been placed on the table by one of our staff. The large white manila envelope has the logo of my father-in-law's attorney's firm on it. The company everyone knows is responsible for the legal affairs of the Larussios. I open the document Carlos put together before his accident and can't help but wonder if he knew that someone would order the hit. I absorb page after page of the single-spaced typed document until I have read every word of the ten pages, and then I start over and begin making notes.

Carlos has been steadfast in his plan not only to secure the most prestigious area on the Strip, but to create the most luxurious casino resorts in all of Vegas and anywhere in the world. It's no secret that his uncle is highly opposed, even though when the property is finished, it will be highly sought after by every high roller across the globe, raising the bar for all other luxury resorts of this type.

I drink my coffee and continue to read over the beneficiary list Carlos has outlined. I reread the paragraph again and again. No one in that family would have any reason to want Carlos dead when he ensures money is funneled through the organization to care for the entire family in New York and abroad, except Giovanni, if he wanted it for himself.

I hit Jay's cell, and my head of security picks up after only one ring. "Jay here," he says.

"Can you get intel to run a background on Giovanni Larussio? I need everything they can find on this man."

"Yep, I can have them start on it right away. You looking for anything in particular?" Jay asks.

"Let's put it this way. If Karissa and Carlos are deceased, he stands to gain half of the entire Larussio Empire," I say.

Jay whistles. "Damn, that's a helluva lot of motive," he says.

"That's exactly what I was thinking. Get a team on it as soon as possible. We need to be prepared for another attack and understand where it's coming from," I say.

"Roger that, I'll get back to you," Jay says before disconnecting.

I hit my cell and connect with Anthony, the attorney who personally manages Carlos's accounts. "Giovanni Larussio is named as one of the beneficiaries if something were to happen to Carlos. Who is this guy?"

"Hello to you, too. I take it you've read the documents I sent over?" Anthony says, but I am in no mood for small talk.

"I have, and I need answers quick," I say.

"Very well, Giovanni Larussio, most often referred to as Gio, is Carlos's nephew. His parents were killed in a car accident quite a few years ago, and his great-uncle took him in and raised him. I looked that much up when I saw the living will, but that's really all I know about him except that he's worth billions. He has luxury resorts all over the globe, along with a multitude of other investments," Anthony says.

"Thank you," I say, keeping the fact that I have my intel looking into his background to myself, at least for now, but text Jay to investigate the car accident of his parents. The fact that his parents were killed the same way that Karissa and Carlos were intended to die does not sit well, and I send another message to Jay to have the men work double time if necessary to get that information into my hands ASAP.

Chapter 6

Gio

My hand is wrapped around Serena's waist, and the silkiness of her long dark hair caresses my skin as it falls over my arm. She's so close that I can smell the minty scent of her mouth, the aroma of delicate floral perfume, and feel the warmth of her breath as it brushes my skin when she inhales and exhales. The thought of those naturally red lips sucking on my dick while that dark blanket of hair falls around her makes my cock throb, and I know if she were an inch closer she would be able to feel the hard-on in my pants. She knows who I am, who my family is, and I can sense the fear emanating from her throughout the entire cabin.

I've asked her to sit, but she remains standing, looking up at me with those velvety brown eyes. My cock hardens as the caress of her breath crosses the skin of my chest and at the fact that she may be the first woman that has not obeyed me immediately when given a command.

"Sweetheart, I asked you to take a seat," I say, patting the bar stool next to me.

She looks at it and then up at me and her breath hitches, but still, she does not move. I take matters into my own hands, picking her up by the waist and placing her on the seat. "If you know who I am, you also know I always get what I want," I say.

Her eyes widen, and I feel her slight body shiver. Damn! It was not my intent to scare her, and I caress her cheek, hoping to calm her, although the thought of her shivering for an entirely different reason makes my cock harder. "Serena, you have nothing to fear. My uncle and I will be in America for a meeting. Instead of going to the hotel when we land, I would like you to accompany us and make sure he is comfortable. You will then travel back to Italy with us when our business concludes."

I feel her entire body relax and I give her a smile, but she shakes her head. "I don't believe I'm the person that you want to care for your great-uncle," Serena says softly.

I straighten to my full height and tilt her chin so that she is looking into my eyes. I was hoping for a different response, but no matter. We can get there a few different ways. "I can call the agency and see if they can fly someone over to assist," I say.

Her lips purse at my suggestion. "My company will not do that when both Brigett and I are available. They will only ask that either of us do this. Why not take Brigett?" Serena asks.

She would prefer I spend time with Brigett than herself, and I find that disappointing. "Brigett did not make such a wonderful merenda for my great-uncle, and he will find her offensive," I say, immediately rewarded with a brief flash of gold that flickers within those velvety brown eyes, but then her lips draw into a firmly set line.

My finger wants to inch from her chin to her lips, caressing them, feeling the softness and the warmth, but I restrain myself, instead removing my finger from her delicate skin.

"If I had known that was going to land me into another job for you and your family, I wouldn't have bothered," Serena huffs.

The chuckle I try to contain barrels forward, and she scowls, the little lines between her eyes crinkling with the effort. No one speaks to a Larussio in this manner, and I should probably make sure she knows this before my uncle awakens. "Did we not already discuss respect? A good old-fashioned spanking over my lap may change your tone, yes?" I say.

She opens her mouth and throws her hands in the air to emphasize a retort, but my finger reaches her lips, silencing the words before they come out.

"The work will only be for a day, and potentially the evening at the hotel before we travel home. We need to attend a business meeting and then visit a family member. I want to make sure my great-uncle is comfortable. He will not be coddled by me and will take great offense if I hire someone for him. As far as anyone else knows, you are hired to take care of my needs," I say.

Her eyes widen. The pulse in her neck is beating rapidly, but her voice is gentle, barely a whisper. "I will take care of your great-uncle until we return home," Serena says, and a twinge of remorse hits me. She really does not want to do this but feels her job is at risk otherwise, and I feel a pang of real guilt.

"Serena, you can say no. I will find someone else, but if you agree to be my personal assistant during this time, I will pay you four times what you were offered to take the last-minute flight, in addition to what the company pays you," I say, looking down into her upturned face as she processes what I've offered.

She nods, and a little sigh of resignation escapes her lips. "It is a very generous offer, Mr. Larussio, and the money would be put to good use," Serena says.

"So you will accept it, and our agreement stands. As far as

anyone else knows, I have hired you to take care of my clerical needs, not my uncle's needs, understand?" I say.

"Yes, Mr. Lar . . ."

"It's Gio when we're alone," I say and am rewarded with a parting of her lips, framing beautiful bright white teeth. "Thank you for helping me," I say and see the tenseness in her small frame begin to relax, and for some reason, I find that extremely pleasing.

"You are welcome, Gio," Serena says softly, and my cock throbs at the sound of my name on her beautiful lips.

"We should discuss a few things. When my uncle wakes, I will introduce you both and let him know that I've hired you as my personal assistant. He's been harping on me to do this for some time to help with the workload, so should be pleased," I say. "Give me your cell phone, and I'll put my number into it."

Serena looks hesitant, but I take it from her dainty hands and place my name and number in her contacts and send a message to myself to ensure I have her number in my own before handing it back to her.

"I prefer to send you messages rather than push the damn button on the remote when I want to communicate with you. There are two rules you need to remember. Make no mention of my great-uncle's name on the phone, messages, or conversation. Simply answer my questions or ask me one in a way that does not use his name," I say, knowing full well that I shouldn't have given her my number and instead waited until security could give me a burner, but the desire to be connected with her is almost primal.

"I probably won't even use it," Serena says, shrugging, and my eyebrows rise with a challenge. Oh, she'll use it alright because rule number two just changed.

"Tesoro, rule number two is that I want to hear from you when I message, understand?" I say, smirking when the little fleck of gold dances back into those deep brown eyes, and she purses those beautifully pouty lips of hers at me. The way she does that makes my cock throb with the thought of her gorgeous lips wrapping around me.

"I'll respond," Serena huffs, glancing at her watch and then down at the floor from her seat.

"Good, then let's get you down. I've kept you long enough," I say, sliding my hands around Serena's taught little waist and placing her on the floor. She blushes crimson and doesn't look me in the eyes, but instead lowers her gaze and my cock throbs hard. I am just about to say something about her submissive tendencies when my great-uncle opens the door from the bedroom he has been napping in.

He eyes her with sleepy suspicion. I'm used to his glare, but she is not, and her anxiety is palpable, and her body tenses. "I'm glad you're awake," I say, turning toward him. "This is Serena, she's my new personal assistant and will be with us for the duration of the trip," I say.

His dark eyes take her in, narrowing to slits, but he is almost polite, extending her a brief greeting.

"Serena, thanks for bringing in the snack. I'll message you later," I say, smiling widely at her, hoping to set her at ease, but she is still visibly tense and scurries toward the door to make her escape.

Dammit, we're right back to where we were with her, on edge and scared.

"Who is she, and why hasn't she been cleared through the appropriate channels, Giovanni?" my great-uncle asks.

It's my turn to scowl. "Her name is Serena, and how do you know she hasn't been?" I ask.

He narrows his eyes at me and doesn't acknowledge my question with a response. The same way he knows everything. "It was a last-minute decision, and the arrangement is only until we return home. I need someone that can take care of the little things so I have time to spend with Uncle Carlos and deal with Katarina," I say.

"Send through the proper clearance, Giovanni. You can never be too certain, understand?"

I nod, knowing that if this plane hadn't been entirely swept by our intel crew, we wouldn't be on it. The risks to the family are too significant. "Yes, it will be done," I say, settling into one of the recliners by the window while he takes the other and begins listening to his voicemails while indulging in the appetizers that Serena has made.

I open my laptop and begin reading the twenty-page document that has been sent to my email. A comprehensive background check and summary of Katarina's life as far back as the investigators can go. I settle in to read everything there is to know about Karissa, Carlos's estranged wife, and the daughter she brought into the world. While the majority of the family have met Katarina on a couple of occasions and were complimentary, even pleased with her desire to become accustomed to our cultures, I have not seen evidence that she is his daughter.

The ladies did not fail to fill me in on the striking similarity Katarina had to her mother when she was at that age, but not once has anyone commented that she looks like a Larussio, no paternity test on file, just Karissa's word. The same woman who walked out on my uncle, leaving him beside himself with grief, is not someone I trust, and her word in this is not nearly enough.

I spend the next two hours reading about the multiple moves Karissa made in her professional life. She used several names at different times, and it was relatively easy for them to track her jobs, payments, and bank accounts after learning what her aliases were. I shake my head at the paltry amount of money she made at each of her many positions, and the numerous schools that Katarina was enrolled in growing up.

I read and then carefully reread the summary of Katarina's high school information, impressed with her academic achievements gaining her scholarships, although not near enough to pay for tuition, room, board, or meals. She took out student loans and worked part-time-plus at the Torzial Consulting firm and still managed to graduate with the highest of honors.

I rifle through a few pages back, and then finally make the connection. Jenny Torzial, her best friend, was her employer even back then, and it appears she still is. Jenny is the very same person that only yesterday was exonerated in a very public court of charges for killing her abusive fiancée. The same woman that owns the very company the Chicago Mafia was running their illegal funds through, and Katarina has been working there for years, the same company that has ties to the fucking Chicago Mafiosi.

I need a break. My uncle is engrossed in his work, and my thoughts travel back to the beautiful submissive young woman who I have convinced to be my personal assistant. I smirk, sending her a message to see if she remembers our rules.

Chapter 7

Serena

I manage to make my way through the service quarter door, kick off my shoes, slumping into the recliner, hugging my knees tightly to my chest as the reality of what I've done sinks in and the trembling begins. I am working for the Italian Mafiosi, the most revered and feared family in my land. The ones I've learned so much about throughout the years. Nonna has told me the stories, the reason we stay well away from them. I cross my heart thoughtfully, and inhale deeply, focusing on my breathing to steady my racing heart after having those evil eyes narrowed at me.

In one hour I have not only managed to allow myself to be talked into working for them, but for money. Money! There is no way that I can explain this to Nonna that will be okay. Time after time, lesson after lesson, did I not hear her warnings and learn from the mistakes of the past?

I hit the button that will connect me to her, just needing to hear her voice, but it goes directly to the voicemail that I have recorded for her. I disconnect, shivering at Nonna's reaction to me being anywhere close to Giovanni or anyone in his family. I think of all the arguments, the ones that led me to accept his offer, but it always comes back to one thing. If I didn't need the stinking job or the money, then I could turn down his offer, walk away, and go to my hotel room until they return home.

If she ever learns my agreement to work for the family was for money to take care of her, it will break her heart. Just the fact that I'm working for them in any capacity will do just that. I could tell Gio that I've changed my mind, and he would probably accept that, but we need the money. He hasn't asked me to do anything illegal, merely provide the same service that I do while in the air: see to their comfort, meals, errands and such. I wipe an errant tear away in frustration. I've made my decision, and I am not changing my mind. We need the money, and Nonna will never know her precious granddaughter has taken money from the Mafiosi. Never!

I busy myself preparing the evening meal, and still not one sign of that lazy Brigett! She is absolutely infuriating, and I really should turn her in, but the simple truth is when partnered with her, I can enjoy the solitude of the trip while she is friendly with the passengers. But she could at least help a little, especially during the busier times.

The swooshing sound on my phone alerts me to an incoming message on my phone, and I go to it.

Uncle has enjoyed the treats. Perhaps a glass of red before dinner?

"Of course I will serve the wine before dinner. I am Italian," I say aloud, raising my hands in the air to gesture my frustration at the arrogance of this man. I glance at the clock and acknowledge that perhaps it is past time to go and check on them, maybe offer them a drink.

I know from his rules that he will expect a reply. "Tesoro, rule number two is that I want to hear from you when I message, understand?" Arrogance, just so arrogant, but the way he called me sweetheart in our native tongue was like a caress, making me shiver, and when he mentioned spanking me, talking to me about something so intimate while holding my eyes captive by his deep brown ones, my pussy moistened and responded with a mind of its own.

I shake my head in denial. I cannot be attracted to this man. The cell phone, it is too personal. He has a remote control, for crying out loud! One that sounds bells and lights to get my attention, and I draw the line at being summoned on my personal device! I toss it on the counter in frustration, knowing it was a mistake to have allowed him my number or agreed to his stupid rules.

The dessert for later this evening is almost finished when a voice behind me, so quiet but deep, makes me almost jump right out of my skin. "Serena, you've already disobeyed my rules, and such simple ones at that," Gio tsks, the husky velvetiness of his voice sending a shiver straight down my spine as the door clicks closed behind him.

I inhale deeply, trying to calm my nerves to face him, ready to give him the spiel I've mentally rehearsed, but as soon as he looks at me, his brows furrow, he scowls and stalks forward. His fingers gently stroke underneath my eye. "You've been crying, Serena," Gio says, looking at the faint black smudge left on his fingers from wiping my skin. "Tell me why, Tesoro," he says, caressing my cheek once again and penetrating me with those inquiring eyes.

I've been warned and should be scared half to death, but my body is thrumming with the excitement of his touch. The way he's looking at me, gentle, like my tears are a concern to him softens my resolve. He has been generous, offering me more than a fair wage, and deserves my honesty. "I was having second thoughts about agreeing to help you, but I've worked through it. It's a substantial offer that I'm hardly in a financial position to turn down," I say.

He says nothing for a moment, seemingly contemplating, and the silence while he assesses me is unnerving. "I see, so you've decided that you can work for the family, but not follow my rules, yes?" Gio says.

He sees too much, and it leaves my lips dry, but I will not lie, even if he decides the arrangement will not work. "I thought better of giving you my personal cell phone. Perhaps we can just continue to use the remote. It alerts me that you need something, and I'm used to it," I say.

His lips turn upward, and his eyes twinkle. "So, you didn't respond intentionally, even though you already agreed to follow my rules, and you didn't think it advisable to discuss it with me first, instead simply ignoring my message altogether?" Gio asks, smirking as he looks down at me.

"Something like that," I say, looking at the floor, anywhere else but at those penetrating eyes that seem to see right through me.

"Serena, look at me, Tesoro," Gio says, gently lifting my chin so that my eyes connect with his deep brown challenging ones. "It was exactly like that, yes?" he asks.

It was childish and ill-mannered and could have been handled in a multitude of ways, and I am adult enough to admit it. "You're right, and I'm sorry. It was rude and quite disrespectful," I say.

"Indeed, we did already discuss respect, yes?" Gio asks, watching me intently, his eyes boring into my own while my cheeks heat and my pussy clenches at the mere thought of how it would feel to have his hand on my upturned bottom while lying across his lap.

"We did, and I apologized," I say, rubbing my bare toes against the satiny carpet and peeking up to glance at him.

He smirks, and his eyes light up. "And you think an apology for such behavior should be enough to avoid a spanking?" Gio asks.

I will never give him the satisfaction of knowing how hot that makes me. "Of course, we are adults. I'm not a child that requires reprimanding. I actually take offense at what you are suggesting that—that you would want to do me harm," I say, stammering for words.

I look up mesmerized by his gaze, aroused by the dark brown eyes capturing mine. Impossible! As attracted to him as I find myself, our lives, our history will not allow it.

He is Mafioso and maybe not the boss, and has made legal entrepreneurship, but Nonna has taught me well. The Family is always the Family.

Chapter 8

Katarina

The ping of the overhead sound system alerts us to an incoming announcement. "Alexis from Salon Diva, here for Katarina," Gaby says over the loudspeaker.

"Please send her up. Katarina is ready," Chase says, shaking hands with our attorney, who has just spent the last forty-five minutes advising me on what I should and should not discuss at the meeting with my great-uncle.

We are sitting at the large mahogany dining room table, and the door opens. A medium-height woman with collar-length blonde curls and deep blue, almost violet eyes is shown into the suite. "Alexis from Salon Diva," Sheldon says, introducing her.

"Nice to meet you," Chase says, extending his hand in greeting. "This is my wife, Katarina, and I'm Chase. Thanks for coming on such short notice. Katarina has an important meeting, and in the event there are cameras, we want to make sure she is prepared," Chase says.

She nods, and her blonde curls bob. "You are most welcome. Katarina, your hair and skin are beautiful, so just a quick style and makeup should work. Plug this in for me, please?" Alexis says, handing Sheldon a plug to a large spiral wand. "Your hair looks naturally curly, let's just go with that, but with sleekness and smoothness, unless you're looking for a different style," Alexis says to me.

"I already put smoother on it, but haven't had a chance to dry it yet," I say.

"We'll have you ready for this meeting in no time at all," Alexis says, handing Sheldon the plug to her blow-dryer and gesturing with her finger to the outlet behind him.

I catch his upturned brow and Chase's wide smile. My husband is having entirely too much fun at Sheldon's expense.

"Okay, let's get you dry real quick. This baby really smokes," Alexis says, turning it on full blast, running its warmth over my hair.

In a matter of ten minutes, my hair is dry and she has applied a product and has started curling my hair with the ceramic wand. She carefully wraps each section tightly, heating them into long spiral curls until she is done with all of my hair. "You like?" Alexis asks, putting a mirror in front of me and spinning me so I can see the back, too.

"Oh my God, yes! I've never seen my hair so curly, glossy, and smooth at the same time," I say, stunned by its quick transformation.

"Just wait, let's powder your face with a mineral base, it will get rid of any extra shine the camera's produce. You have such beautiful skin, nothing else is essential, unless you want me to give you extra color to your cheeks and a bit of glam," Alexis says.

"Maybe just a little," I say, raising my fingers to gesture just a pinch, catching Chase's amusement in the mirror.

She laughs. "Very good, let's boost you with a little apricot coloring, apply a thin coat of eyeliner on top, just enough to enhance, and then voilà, we finish with a ginger lip gloss," Alexis says, nodding her head emphatically, causing her blonde curls to bounce. "You were absolutely beautiful already, but this will help against the harsh lights of the camera," Alexis says, admiring her handy work.

I start to stand up, but she presses on my shoulder.

"Not so fast. Let me fluff your curls," she says laughing, fingering the spiral curls that are now set, spreading them apart with her fingers to add more fullness and bounce. "There, how do you like it?" Alexis asks, spinning me in the chair again so this time I'm facing the mirror.

"I absolutely love it! You're amazing! Thank you," I say, honestly not recognizing my hair or flawless looking skin.

She laughs and smiles widely. "You are more than welcome. It was a pleasure to work with you," Alexis says, leaning over to unplug the iron and blow-dryer.

She goes to slide them into her case, and Sheldon reaches out to take them from her. "Shouldn't you cool them off first?" he asks.

Alexis smiles, her bright white teeth gleaming against the deep coral color of her lipstick. "Heat resistant bag," she says, winking at Sheldon before packing them into her travel bag.

"I love how my hair looks. Do you have a card from your salon?" I ask.

She rummages through her purse and hands me one as Sheldon's phone swooshes with a text message.

"We need to get you to Prestian Corp and Alexis back to the salon," Sheldon says, and I know the concerned look that's on his face right now. "Chase, make sure that Kate gets ready in less than ten minutes. I'll work with the security team to ensure transportation to Prestian Corp is seamless. In the meantime, I'm going to assign someone to see Alexis home," Sheldon says.

"That's such a sweet offer, but I'm perfectly fine to see myself home. I drove here in my own car," Alexis says.

"Exactly the reason you're not going home the same way. Someone will escort you home, and then I'll return your car to you later. Just routine security precautions," Sheldon says.

Her lips purse, and I see her eyes roll and his eyes narrow as he catches sight of it.

"It's for your protection. We don't have time to argue about it. I'll walk you out," Sheldon says.

Chase is doing his best to conceal a grin. "I'll make sure Katarina is ready when you return," he says, taking my hand as we walk upstairs.

"What was that all about?" I ask, never having seen Sheldon with a woman before.

"Hard to say, Baby," Chase says, his lips curling up in a smile as he looks at me.

It takes me less than six minutes to shimmy into the outfit that I've already tried on. The one that will make me feel confident enough to face the very person that put the hit out on my parents. I twirl in front of the floor-to-ceiling mirror, taking in the outfit. It reminds me of all the right things: the color of dice, Las Vegas, the legacy we are fighting for, and it couldn't be more perfect.

Chase spins me around. "You are breathtaking, and look intimidating, just like you did when you visited Vicenti. When you met with him, you had the duration of the trip to Brazil to psych yourself up for the conversation, determine what you would say, how you would say it, and how you would react to specific questions. Have you been thinking about how you'll navigate this conversation?" Chase asks, pulling me closer, grasping my nape beneath my hair in his hands.

"I've been thinking about almost nothing else since I learned that I had to meet him," I say.

"Remember, he wants to discredit you, so be guarded. Your mother went underground for twenty-three years for a reason. We can't be sure this family didn't put a hit out on your parents. You'll be wearing a wire, and it will give our attorney time to listen to the conversation and replay it later if needed."

"I should be petrified, but I'm not. I'm finally going to meet the head of the Italian Mafia, my own great-uncle, the one that wants my father and mother out of the picture so he can take over the investments that my dad made to ensure our family's long-term security in the future," I say.

Chase pulls me tighter to his chest. "I have no doubt that you have this completely under control, but we need to go," he says, guiding me to the elevator and to the limo that is waiting to take us to the Prestian Corp skyrise.

Chapter 9

Chase

The traffic is hellacious, but our driver navigates it with skill and patience and in less than forty minutes has pulled up alongside the looming Prestian Corp skyrise, one of the most prestigious and tallest structures in New York City, looming tall and boasting of steel and glass overlooking Manhattan.

The security team surrounds us as we make our way inside the building and into the private elevator that will take us to the administrative area adjacent to my office. The door opens into our spacious contemporary waiting area, and one of the receptionists on duty greets us warmly, letting us know the Larussios from Italy have arrived and are in the conference room waiting for us.

I place my hand on the small of Katarina's back, guiding her forward, and pull her close as the security team scans the area and gives me the green light. "You will do great. Remember, Baby, you're holding all the cards right now," I whisper into her ear.

Katarina nods, and I feel her inhale deeply. Her father has entrusted her with the family legacy, and I have no doubt that she will navigate this to the letter, but damn if I don't want her anywhere but here. These people could snuff her life out without any advance warning.

I open the door, my hand on her back, allowing her to walk in first, knowing she will make an impression. Two men are seated at the long oval mahogany table. The older man I recognize from pictures that I have been researching. His dark hair is almost completely turned to a silvery grey, but his deep brown eyes are penetrating and surprisingly warm as he gazes at my wife. The notorious great-uncle, finally, we are face-to-face. He walks around the table to greet us. "Katarina Prestian Larussio, it is a delight to meet you in person," he says, extending his hand to the top of Katarina's shoulders, bringing her in for a kiss, first on the right, then on the left. She has studied our culture, and I am proud of her reciprocation.

"Likewise, I'm sorry you weren't able to attend the wedding. I was looking forward to meeting you and all of my family," Katarina says, as the other younger man with him stands.

"Ah, yes, prior commitments, otherwise nothing would have prevented me from meeting my grand-niece," the older man says, before shaking hands with me. "An honor to meet the son of Don Prestian."

"Very nice to meet you also, sir," I say, addressing her great-uncle, and squeezing her hand before leaving to stand beside Sheldon. We have every security precaution imaginable in place and backups just in case, but knowing that my wife is the only thing in the way of the two men in this room controlling the entire Larussio fortune has turned my blood cold.

I watch as she studies her great-uncle. He looks slightly older than I envisioned, with olive-colored skin that is weathered from age and sun. His eyes, though, they are sharp, but they are not watching her every move and penetrating hers like the tall, dark, and handsome man standing beside him. I recognize him from the pictures our intel has provided.

"This is my great-nephew, your cousin, Giovanni Larussio," her great-uncle says, introducing the tall dark-haired man with brown brooding eyes that has stood up to shake hands with everyone around the room, and finally, lastly, extends it to Katarina instead of a hug and kiss.

I raise my eyebrows, surprised that he's broken custom and been so rude. The scowl that Katarina's great-uncle gives him lets me know he's not pleased with the greeting either.

Clearly, Katarina notices as well. "Please, have a seat gentleman," she says, standing at the head of the table, and they all do what she asks at the very same time as Katarina sits and engages the intercom. "Cassandra, would you please bring in a pot of tea with a pitcher of ice water?" she asks.

"Yes, Mrs. Prestian," Cassandra replies.

"Thank you," she says, disconnecting.

Her great-uncle's eyebrows raise, assessing her.

"I appreciate you making the trip to the United States. While we could have met via phone or Skype. It means a lot that you would travel so far to meet me," Katarina says, and I know she's being gracious and gauging where this conversation heads.

"I wouldn't have it any other way. I do feel bad for not being at your wedding. The family members spoke highly of you," her great-uncle says.

His dark-eyed stare makes her uneasy. She appears unnerved, but her dainty fingers that rub the inside of her palm, hidden to them by the table, tell me different. I vowed to let her handle this, but it is with at an extreme cost to me personally, and my jaw clenches tightly. "If I recall you weren't at the meeting my father requested when he first learned I was his daughter and my mother was kidnapped, either," Katarina says, and I grimace. Her emotions may be getting the better of her, and I look to Sheldon to make sure he's on the ready.

A spark of surprise registers in her great-uncle's dark eyes at being called out this way, and he appears thoughtful for a moment. "So you don't do what the Americans say, beat around the bush, no?" he says, and I smirk waiting for my baby's response as Giovanni's eyebrows raise.

"I find it quite a waste of emotional energy," Katarina says.

"Very well, but you are looking for a reason, no?" her great-uncle says, still watching intently.

"It would be helpful to hear why you felt inclined not to meet your nephew's only daughter and welcome her into the family when everyone else did—well, except a few," she says, looking pointedly into Giovanni's watchful eyes. "I didn't even know I had a family, then learned of one, and they couldn't be bothered to show up. It still hurts, and I'm not going to pretend that it doesn't," Katarina says.

"Your father and I have different visions for the family, hence the visit today," her great-uncle says.

"I appreciate your honesty. That's something I can understand, but the family is family," Katarina says.

He nods slowly, contemplating his response. "You are right, and I owe you an apology," and Giovanni's eyebrows raise in surprise. "I would like to get to know you better, Katarina. I'm sorry that I made you feel slighted by my distance, but maybe we can put that behind us now."

She smiles at him. "I believe in the interest of the family's future we should do precisely that," Katarina says just as Cassandra comes in with the tray of refreshments she requested.

Cassandra pours the tea, dropping a wedge of the lemon into the cup and fills a crystal glass full of ice water before placing it in front of Katarina, as though she knows exactly how she likes it.

Cassandra does not ask our guests their preference, but instead pours them the same drink and places one in front of Katarina's great-uncle as she has been instructed to do before moving onto Giovanni.

I see Katarina smile slightly, feeling a small moment of victory, and notice the flicker of annoyance pass across her great-uncle's countenance at not being asked for his choice, but to his credit, he hides it quickly, thanking Cassandra before she leaves the room. I glance up and see the upturned lips of Giovanni Larussio. He looks smug and arrogant, but obviously amused, enjoying this exchange.

Katarina has never been one for monetary trinkets, instead treasuring all the gifts I've given her as tokens of what they mean in our relationship, and I love that about her. At this particular moment, though, I know that she is appreciative of her perfectly manicured fingers, of the five-carat diamond ring that sits on her finger, and the silver and diamond bangles and necklace that adorn her skin. It helps her get into the part, to play the mafia boss's daughter, and I make a mental note to buy her a few more trinkets in the future.

She toys with the edge of her crystal glass, swirling the lemon in her water, drawing her great-uncle's eyes to the jewelry which adorns her finger and wrists. He is a man accustomed to luxury and knows at a glance the magnitude of the money I spend on her jewelry, and that in itself gives her the power and confidence to go against someone so formidable.

"So maybe we can start by you telling me a little bit about yourself," her great-uncle says, toying with the glass in front of him.

She brings her own to her lips, takes a sip, letting him know with that one move we haven't poisoned his drink. He lifts his glass in salute. "My mother left my father twenty-three years ago, not knowing she was pregnant with me. I grew up without a father and without roots. It was only by chance that I learned my father was alive and that I had a family," Katarina says, and I know personally what that has cost her emotionally.

Her great-uncle studies her for a few moments, and I feel the full force of his deep brown eyes penetrating her, and watch as her fingers rub her palm. "I'm sure it must have been difficult growing up without a papa, Katarina, and I am sincerely happy that you have been brought into our fold. It is not you that I take issue with, please know that," her great-uncle says.

She nods, but I know she is not about to be taken in by deception while her father is still fighting for his life. "I appreciate that. It means a great deal to me, but I need to better understand what it is that you do take issue with. My father has spent the last twenty-three years of his life saving, investing in legal properties and ventures that will allow him to take care of his family well into the future. I would think that, as the eldest member of the family, you would be pleased, but I don't think that's the case. I honestly don't understand," Katarina says, knowing she's going off script, prying, when instead our intel unit wanted to find out what they wanted to learn from her.

"After the family came to visit you, they reported back that they thought you had a good heart, loved your husband immensely, and were committed to our family. I see what they saw, and am already gaining great respect for your honesty and integrity, Katarina," her great-uncle says.

"I am completely committed to our family, and like my father and yourself, invested in their future. However, we have different opinions on how we might sustain that in the future," Katarina says, taking a sip of her tea.

"It is true, and you are not only perceptive but forthright to bring the discussion into the open. You have strengths and capabilities that I did not see, that your father did, and they are most pleasing to me," her great-uncle says.

"Thank you, that is very kind," she says.

"One thing you will learn about me Katarina is that I do not give out compliments for the sake of doing so. You are charismatic, open and honest, and have an already deep-seated commitment to the family you've only just met. It's refreshing, and I have to admit that it's not what I expected," he says, watching her intently for a response.

"What did you expect?" Katarina asks, trying to avoid the penetrating gaze of Giovanni's dark eyes glaring at her. Sheldon notices, too, and is tense beside me, on the ready if trouble breaks out.

"If I'm honest, a young woman that found her way into a wealthy family. Someone able to worm their way into the heart of a man that found himself with a daughter after years of pining away after her mother. What I did not expect, however, was someone that due to no fault of their own, found themselves without a family and is deeply committed to ensuring their long-term success and viability in the future. That is what we need to discuss," her great-uncle says, taking another sip of his lemon water.

"Well, I appreciate your honesty if not your initial thoughts of me. I am more than happy to share the plans for the Vegas build with you. In fact, why don't we do that right now," Katarina says, hitting the buttons on the remote control that bring the blinds down over the floor-to-ceiling windows, and further dims the light in the room.

I smirk. My baby's so got this. Showtime!

Chapter 10

Gio

I knew the very first time Serena looked at me that she realized exactly who I am. Her fear was palpable, and I have come to expect it as people recognize me, but for some reason had hoped that it would have dissipated somewhat after our conversation.

She knows who and what this family is, and it's not something she wants to be a part of. All the women I've met throw themselves at me looking for the wealth, status, and power our family name brings, but not her. Those are precisely the things she's trying to avoid and for some reason that just makes me want her even more, and I restrain myself, but only because my uncle would see too much.

She serves our dinner, and then comes back into the main cabin an hour or so later to make sure we have everything we need, but she keeps her eyes lowered, avoiding my eyes as she goes about her business, and then heads back to her cabin.

It is with immense control that I wait until my great-uncle retires before seeking out my naughty little minx. I find her standing by the counter, stirring a creamy batter. Her sweater is laying over the back of a nearby chair, and she is barefoot. I walk in, calling her name so as not to scare her.

"Tesoro, you have me all wrong. I might want to hurt you a little bit, but only in a way that will please you until you are screaming my name, again and again, and again," I say as she turns and I stroke her cheek.

Her eyes grow wide, and momentarily I'm almost sorry I've said this aloud, until her eyes dilate and the pulse in her neck begins to beat more rapidly. I don't even think she realizes that she leans into my touch, lightly nuzzling against the fingers that are still gently caressing her cheek. She has no idea how utterly perfect that she is.

"Serena, if you don't want to work for me, you only need to say so. I'll find someone else," I say, knowing that if she takes the out I've offered, I will regret having provided it.

The rise of her full eyebrows and the little shake of her head bring me only a small sense of relief. "It was extremely generous, and I want to help you, but . . ." Serena says, pausing, chewing her lip, and apparently still contemplating her response.

"But what? Tell me," I say, lifting her chin with the tip of my finger so those gorgeous eyes have nowhere else to go except to look into my own, exactly where I want them.

She runs the tip of her tongue along the seam of her beautifully parted lips. I swallow hard at the sight and pre-cum leaks from the head of my cock. Fuck, everything about this woman makes my blood race. She licks her lips again, and my cock expands painfully, pushing against the zipper of my pants, forcing me to shift to get some relief.

Her eyes lower, and that tells me exactly what I need to know. Whatever she's contemplating is not something she believes will please me, and I know without a doubt that it must stem from her fear of our family name and legacy. No sweet girl like her would want to socialize with one of us, but that doesn't stop me from wanting to feel her body pressed up against my own, to slide her skirt up over her luscious ass and part her legs so that I can taste her. I look down into those eyes that are as glazed over with longing as I believe my own to be.

"Tell me what you're afraid of, and I expect the truth, Serena," I say.

She looks up and into my eyes as her tongue runs along her lower lip, still hesitant and contemplating, but with no further coaxing, answers my question. "Once I do this, will the job be done, or will I be indebted to you or to your family?" Serena asks, her eyes full of concern and an honest sincerity that I both admire and find refreshing.

She's smart and must know exactly how the family has controlled people throughout the years. The thought of her working for anyone else in the family, dealing with my cousins in any way shape or form makes my blood run cold. "You work only for me, Serena, only me, and our agreement stands, just until we get back to Italy. Then you go back to your life," I say.

She looks up at me, contemplating this for a few moments before she nods her agreement.

I swallow hard, because the offer I've made rings false for so many reasons, even to my own ears. I don't get involved with a lady any further than it takes to get her into my bed, but something about this woman makes me want to take her into my arms and protect her.

She tilts her head and looks up at me, those seductive deep brown eyes gazing into my own as she nods, and her long black hair spills over her shapely frame. I angle her chin so that I can look into her eyes. They are full of emotion and filled with a longing that I fully intend to satisfy. I run my hands through those silky strands of hair, cradling her nape and pulling her toward me. Her eyes dilate, and the pulse in her neck quickens as I capture her lips, parting them so I can explore and taste her sweetness with my tongue. She moans as I pull her roughly against me, grasping her hips in my hands, lifting her and setting her on the counter.

"Tesoro, let me pleasure you," I say, kissing her while I begin to unbutton her blouse, one pearl button at a time, feeling the creaminess of her delicate skin as I go. I relinquish her lips and kiss and suck down the length of her long graceful neck as I push her blouse from her shoulders. She purrs with pleasure as I caress her nipples with my fingers, teasing them through the lacy material of her bra. I suckle her in the sensitive spot between her neck and shoulder while I unclasp the clip that keeps her hidden from me.

She inhales sharply as she realizes she is now bare to my gaze, and I inhale at the gorgeously erotic sight before me. Her nipples are erect and dark rose in color against the creaminess of her olive skin. "Jesus, you're gorgeous," I say, caressing the firmness of her peach-sized breasts, savoring the way she pushes into my hands as I roll her nipples between my thumb and finger. I squeeze, a little and then more, testing her desires, what she likes, and with the increased pressure of my touch, she pants and pushes against me. Fuck, so perfect, and my dick hardens painfully at how responsive she is.

I reward Serena by taking her swollen nipples into my mouth, suckling one, and then the other, licking and caressing. My hands slide over the curves of her hips, wrapped in the modest navy blue skirt of her uniform. I fully intend to explore her thighs and make quick work of the material that keeps me from her heat, but her cell phone rings with a whimsical tune, and at the same time, all the passion in her eyes dissipates before me and the fear and unease of earlier returns.

"I'm so sorry. It's my nonna, I have to take it," Serena says, looking guiltily at the phone across the room, reaching for her blouse and placing it around her shoulders to cover herself.

I put my finger to her lip to quiet her worries. The thought of her velvety lips wrapped around my cock makes it throb with need, but I saw the change when the phone rang, and she remembered who she was with. "Shh. No apologies. Go and talk to your nonna," I say, vowing to find out everything there is to know about Serena, before heading to the main cabin.

I pour myself a glass of wine as I pull open the couch that opens into a double bed, and grab a blanket from the drawers below it, undressing and settling in to finish a glass of vino. Everything in Serena's response told me that she wanted me, but as soon as that damn call came in, she looked like the first time I met her. Wide-eyed and scared and dammit, I hate that. My entire life I have been trying to get out from underneath the shadows of my family.

While I'm not ashamed of our heritage, I wanted something different, and I've been successful in my own right, worth billions from legitimate operations, but clearly that will never be enough. I will always be under these shadows as long as I live in Italy and am recognized.

I finish my drink and decide to skim the stocks before trying to get some sleep. I hear the door open quietly, and Serena enters the main cabin. She's now fully dressed, but her feet are still bare, and the tips of her toenails are decorated in a white French tipped design. I try to shake the thoughts about having them wrapped around my neck and look up at her face instead.

"I'm sorry about before. I wasn't trying to lead you on or be promiscuous. It just happened. I don't act like that. Ever," Serena says.

"No need to apologize. What was the call about? Everything okay?" I ask.

"I take care of my nonna, and she's not well. I'm going to need to return home and have someone else assigned to your return trip. I'm really sorry about our arrangement and everything, but I need to be with her," Serena says, as though she needs to explain why getting mixed up with the most notorious crime family in Italy is not reason alone.

"It's not a problem, Serena. I'll have you flown back as soon as we land," I say.

"That's very nice of you. I really appreciate that."

"Of course. Now, you should get some sleep. You've got a long flight and lots to deal with when you get home. Good night, Serena," I say.

She looks at me like she wants to say something else, but doesn't, spinning and closing the door between our cabins, leaving me to contemplate this overwhelming attraction between us as I make plans for her return to Italy.

When we land, security is quick to escort me and my great-uncle to the awaiting limo. I watch the plane as we drive away, hoping for a glimpse of Serena, but the flight crew must still have work to do aboard. I text Antonio to make sure everything is still in place for her return, and he lets me know they will be taking off shortly. Great-uncle makes idle talk on the way to the Prestian Corp building where we are meeting with Chase Prestian and his new wife. Katarina Meilers, my presumed cousin, the one who has already managed to connive her way into his will and only weeks before he was in an accident that not many people would have survived.

The elevator to the Prestian Corp executive suites opens. The receptionist greets us and takes us to a large conference room where we await her arrival. My uncle seems nervous, and I bet that he is. I'm sure he never contemplated that Carlos Larussio would leave his entire fortune to anyone other than the head of the Italian Mafiosi, and certainly not to Katarina and me jointly in this way.

We are not waiting long before she walks in looking like an executive of Prestian Corp rather than the new wife. She clearly knows what she's doing. My uncle greets her with hugs and kisses, but I'm no fool and am not in the mood to play fucking games today.

Chapter 11

Katarina

My great-uncle's pushing all the right buttons, saying all the things that my heart wants to hear. However, at the end of the day, I am my parents' daughter and will not be fooled. I know my father has left me in charge because he doesn't trust the man in front of me. Our intel believes that he or someone in this family gave the order to have a semi-truck drive over the center line and hit them head-on while my father was taking my mother out to celebrate their first-anniversary dinner after being apart for over twenty-three years.

He has no idea what it feels like to see the light go out of your mother's eyes as she suffers through her own pain, not knowing if her husband will survive the accident. No idea what it feels like wondering if my father will die, after having to be placed in a coma and undergoing a procedure that required drilling holes into his skull to relieve the pressure in his brain.

He thinks I'm gullible and soft, but I am not. I stand up, and while not tall, with the help of my Jimmy Choos, I am a formidable five foot eight inches tall. My heels and suit portray a specific image, and I make a mental note to thank Chase for ensuring I have what I need today.

I lean over the table, taking the remote control into my hands, darkening the room and bringing up the presentation I have prepared on the full-wall screen. It is nine minutes in total, clear, concise, and hopefully to the point, providing an overview of what my father's living will outlines, what I am sure they have already been told, but shows them exactly how we intend to ensure it is lived out.

My great-uncle is extremely quiet as he watches the presentation that outlines the vision my father believes will sustain our family in the future.

"The presentation that you just shared with us was well thought-out, Katarina. While I'm sure your intentions are good, and of that, I have no doubt, this is not the direction our family will take in the future."

"You'll have to forgive me being so newly introduced to our family, but when you say our family, do you mean everyone or parts of the family?" I ask, and I see Giovanni's dark eyes light up and the upturned curl of his lips.

My great-uncle narrows his dark-colored eyes at me. I feel his disagreement and passion as he talks. "Katarina, there is history, a responsibility to others that you may or may not know about. We must follow the course," he says, taking another drink of his tea.

I nod. "I appreciate your honesty and assume this path you discuss can be shared with me? I'd like to better understand, especially if it's in direct conflict with the task I've been charged to complete," I say.

He smiles broadly, amusement shining in his dark eyes. "I find you so very candid young lady. I believe sharing the family's vision with you would be most enjoyable, but unfortunately, we need to return home straight away for another meeting. I'm happy to schedule a return visit to review it with you," my great-uncle says as Giovanni's eyebrows raise in surprise.

My great-uncle thinks I'm going to twiddle my thumbs and that the project will sit idle while I wait. Interesting, but he couldn't be more wrong. "I appreciate your willingness to review this with me. Unfortunately, I have some incredibly tight deadlines with the Vegas build already underway that will require my personal attention. I'll need Giovanni's help, as he's been named to ensure operations are implemented," I say.

My great-uncle turns, trying to keep his emotions in check, and while it's clear he's displeased, doesn't look shocked, while Giovanni just seems intrigued by the exchange but says nothing, meeting his uncle's look dead on.

"My husband and I will be flying to Italy and plan to attend the family gathering later in the week. We can meet at your office and save you another trip to the States," I say, twirling my silver and diamond bracelets which give me a bolster of confidence. I need it right now, because the thought of this man in New York, being this close to my mother and father, makes me shiver with apprehension. The farther this man is away from my parents, the better.

I see a flicker of something flash through his eyes, and a slight upward curl of his lips. I'm not sure if it's his way of smiling or an attempt to keep his amusement in check, but I find both scenarios utterly unnerving.

"I should have known my grand-niece, the one with enough fortitude to fly into the enemy's territory without regard for her own life, would be most interesting indeed," my great-uncle says.

I stand and turn slightly, clicking off the overhead projector to show him the meeting is coming to a close and I have more pressing things to do, but also to ensure he does not see my surprise at his statement.

He knows more about me than he should. Very few people not on Chase's payroll are aware of the trip that I took to meet with the head of the South American Cartel, other than a few close friends and the people who assisted us. I make a mental note to have our intel find out how he knew.

My great-uncle stands and Giovanni does likewise. "It's been an honor and a privilege to meet you, Katarina. I look forward to your arrival in our homeland and to sharing the history and vision of our family with you." He reaches into his jacket pocket to retrieve a card. "Contact this number. Carlotta, my personal assistant, will assist you with directions. You and your husband are welcome to stay at the villa. We have a multitude of guest homes on the property, and you can tour the vineyards, if you like," my great-uncle says.

Chase steps forward. "Greatly appreciate the offer, sir, but I haven't yet had an opportunity to show her my home. I've made plans to stay at my villa on the Amalfi Coast for the duration of our trip. It's conveniently located near both your villa and my family's, but we would graciously accept a tour of your vineyards. They are renowned worldwide, and it would be an honor," Chase says.

My great-uncle's eyes light up with appreciation. "Excellent that you plan to spend time with your family. They will be delighted, as will we.

"I look forward to seeing you both at the end of the week," he says, pulling me close and kissing first my right cheek and then my left before Giovanni does the same.

"I look forward to seeing you and our family and learning more about our heritage," I say, in large part because it is what I rehearsed, but also because it is true. I have enjoyed getting to know my family, but that does not mean I will let my guard down, especially since he's made it clear that my father's vision is not the intended path he plans to lead them to.

Sheldon and my great-uncle's security guard guide him and Giovanni out of the room, and I slink into one of the leather chairs after the door closes behind them. "I'm so sorry I went off script! I was just so curious, and angry," I say.

Chase walks toward me and moves my hair from the nape of my neck and bends to kiss me. "You were curious, it was expected and natural. He saw true emotion, not an act, and as a result he will share with you the vision he has for the family. You will learn, Baby, you will understand, and then you will make your decisions," Chase says, massaging my neck with his thumbs and fingers. I do not move and I couldn't if I wanted to. It feels divine, and ten minutes later I am more relaxed than I have been all day.

"Come," Chase says, grasping my hand and guiding me toward the door.

"Where are we going?" I ask.

He stops abruptly and closes the door. "This room is bug proof, but once we leave it we'll need to be careful. Sheldon has the plane ready. We're heading to Italy, Baby," Chase says.

"Whoa, right now? I thought I'd have time to pack and get prepared, you know, psych myself up for it and all," I say.

He smiles, a broad beam meant all for me, and it settles my nerves in an instant, letting me know it's okay and that he's there for me. "You'll have all the time in the world. We're heading back to Bel Air, the opposite direction anyone would expect us to take to Italy. The flights are getting scrambled as we speak, and in a matter of hours we'll be at Brian's, and I'll have you in his lower-level playroom."

Chapter 12

Chase

The copter touches down at the private airstrip, and we are escorted by the security team to the Carrington Gulfstream. Katarina glances at the emblem on the plane in confusion. "We switched jets to stay under the radar," Sheldon says, and my jaw tightens of its own accord, knowing that now she will worry.

The crew members welcome us aboard as I guide Katarina up the ramp and into the contemporarily decorated cabin. Black leather couches situated around a fireplace made of steel and slate, with long oblong-shaped windows. The plane has two doors that lead to the back. I know without exploring them that one will lead us into the main bathroom and one will take us into a master suite.

We get settled into a soft leather seat by the window. "I'm so glad that meeting is over. There's so much swirling around in my mind right now," Katarina says, and I pull her to me, kissing the top of her head.

"You were terrific, Baby. He came here wanting to see you as the enemy, but he couldn't, so now he's left to ponder how to navigate this situation."

"Hmm, what do you make of Giovanni? He didn't say much," she says.

"The verdict's still out. My initial take was rude and arrogant, but something seemed to change for your cousin toward the end," I say, not revealing to my curious little wife that the intel team is currently combing through the details surrounding his parents' death. While he was too young to have caused it years ago, the coincidence of them dying in an accident similar to Katarina's parents is concerning. "Giovanni has done extremely well for himself with dozens of high-end resorts all over the world. Your father clearly knew his operational skills and abilities, or he wouldn't have put him in charge of them at his own resort."

Sheldon walks into the cabin. "Anyone watching will have their eyes on the Prestian Corp plane taking off tomorrow. The flight from New York to Italy has been registered and aligns with the conversation Kate had with her great-uncle today. If they're watching this flight, they're going to assume Brian's men are flying Gaby out to his home in Bel Air," he says.

"Why would they assume that?" Katarina asks.

Sheldon gestures toward the door as Gaby bustles through it. "What!" Katarina squeals, peeling out of her seat to go and hug Gaby's rotund figure as she makes her way into the cabin.

"You didn't think I was going to let you and Chase get away from me that fast, did you?" Gaby says, grinning widely.

"I had no clue you would be coming with! Come on," Katarina says, taking Gaby's hand and pulling her into the loveseat that is adjacent to the fireplace.

I couldn't be happier that the two women who mean the most to me are so close. Gaby has taken care of my homes and me for the last seven years. "Thanks for coming, Gaby," I say, leaving out the fact that for the next week or so we're going to need to make sure everyone we care about is taken care of.

I look to Jay sitting across from me. He's quiet, and contemplating. I glance up, feeling the heat of my wife's inquisitive blue eyes focused on me. She is too smart for her own good. I should tell her that our intel is certain her family is being followed, but until we know by whom, it will add more worry to her already overloaded plate, and if she suspects, she may inadvertently tip our hand.

"I want to check out that service area and see if we can whip up some snacks for the men once we take off," Gaby says, and I grin. The flight attendants won't know what to think of her.

In a matter of minutes, the engines engage and roar, and the sleek silver Gulfstream with the dark blue Carrington Steel emblem lifts into the sky, bypassing all the wonders of Manhattan, leaving Lady Liberty far below as we soar into the clouds.

When we're at a safe altitude, Gaby heads to the galley on a mission. As soon as the door closes to the main cabin, I unbuckle Katarina and take her hand, guiding her to the master suite in the back of the plane.

* * *

She raises her arms as I've asked, allowing me to remove her dress and bra and linger, holding her breasts in my hands, teasing her nipples between my thumb and forefinger, knowing that she feels it right in her center. She's unbuttoning my dress shirt and pushes it from my shoulders, and then her greedy little hands trail down my body to unzip my pants, finding me hardened and ready. I'll let her have some fun, take the lead for a few minutes, but she's not in charge of her pleasure. I am.

"You have the most beautiful body, and it all belongs to me," I say, nipping the tips of her breasts with my teeth before trailing a line of kisses down the length of her waist and sliding her lacy little panties over the curves of her hips and letting them fall to the floor. My tongue finds her navel, and I can feel her belly tighten with desire as I caress it and head lower. I part her gently, breathing in her scent.

She moans softly with pleasure as my tongue caresses her slowly with long lingering strokes. She places her hands on my shoulders, steadying herself as I grasp her hips, slightly increasing the rhythm of my tongue. She tries to move, but I won't allow it, instead slowing my movement, gently caressing and sucking, then repeating the pattern until I know she is close.

Then I lick her lightly, but right off the mark, watching her breathing as she gets right to the edge, just where I want her, before pulling away. Her moan this time is in frustration as the waves fade, but she knows that waiting, the anticipation, will bring far greater pleasure, and I intend to ensure it.

I rub her sensitive bundle of nerves as I pull out the silver-and-diamond clit chain custom designed for her, watching her blue eyes haze over with desire.

"Wearing this for the remainder of the flight and this evening should help you appreciate patience and anticipation," I say, kissing her directly on her sensitive little nub before affixing the jewelry to the most sensitive part of her body. She tenses in anticipation, and her entire body shivers with pleasure as I push the button on the mini-remote and the suction begins.

In seconds the silver jewelry is securely where I want it, and firmly affixed. My tongue caresses the insides of her thighs while making my way to her navel and then back up to her breasts. I kiss each erect nipple, one after another, before licking my way to her collarbone and then the sensitive shell of her neck.

"You're going to make me wait until tonight," she moans, as I kiss the sensitive skin below her ear.

She knows me well but has no idea what occurs in the lower-level playroom of Brian Carrington's mansion. "Indeed, you are in for an extremely long night, Baby."

Chapter 13

Gio

We walk out of the Prestian Corporation and get into the limo that is waiting to take us to Carlos. Uncle is clearly agitated but says nothing for the first ten minutes. I give him time and know that he'll eventually voice his concerns.

When I first saw Katarina walk in, I thought she was a cold-hearted little gold digger. As she was talking about the hurt that came with not growing up with a father or family other than her mother, I was dissecting her features. While she is the spitting image of her mother, I began to ferret out the physical attributes that are clearly from the Larussio side. Her ears, such a funny thing to focus on, but they are identical to my great-uncle's, my own, and many of our family's. Then there are the eyes. While she undeniably has the sparkling blue eyes of her mother, the shape is pure Larussio. Then my favorite, most telling sign of all is that she doesn't even try to win my great-uncle over. She is full of passion and determined to convince our great-uncle of the attributes of her father's dream. I find that more than admirable and will do everything in my power to ensure it comes true for my favorite uncle and his daughter.

We're almost near my uncle's home when my great-uncle turns to me. "Giovanni, Katarina is just like her father, like you. Carlos clearly understands that, which is why he left the two of you his fortune. He always wanted to modernize our world, move away from our heritage. We continue to fight this," my great-uncle says.

"Carlos doesn't want to change our heritage, just be able to provide for the family in a legitimate monetary stream. When I began investing in resorts, I wasn't looking to change the family's history. I did, however, want to figure out how to use the money for good and be able to support myself with legal funds. That desire doesn't mean that we don't believe in the work of the family. Ensuring our communities are protected, going head-to-head with the dealers who would bring poison into our communities instead of a pure product," I say.

He nods slowly. "You and your cousin are very much alike. Katarina's fire reminded me of the day you told me about your plan for the future years ago. That same drive and desire," he says.

"I felt the same way as you after meeting her. I had a background drawn up, and everything checked out. I believe she is who she claims to be and that she is genuinely trying to move forward with Uncle Carlos's wishes. She stood her ground even when you were clearly opposed. She looked for a way to connect with you to continue working forward, but she didn't cave. Any woman that can hold her own with you must be a Larussio," I say.

He shakes his head slowly as our driver pulls up to the heavily guarded gates of the Larussio mansion, home to Carlos Larussio and his wife, Karissa.

Katarina will have her work cut out for her. Our great-uncle will not be easily swayed, but I can tell that she has him thinking, and that alone is a great feat. While he was fine with me venturing into a career of my own, he was not interested in having it be a subsidy for the family's lifestyle. These days, things are more complicated. The families are running entirely legitimate businesses, and I have to admit the plans for The Larussio Resort and Casino and all the amenities I've seen outlined to this point are fantastic and futuristic.

We pull up to the gates of my uncle's home. I thought we had security at home, but it's nothing like this. Armed men surround our car. Try as I might to explain who we are and to get the security guard to call Carlos personally to see if he will receive visitors, it falls on deaf ears, while resolute-looking men with what could be itchy trigger fingers glare at us.

"Dammit! Let's go back home, we'll call him from there," my great-uncle says to our driver, so I text our team to have the jet readied, disappointed that my great-uncle may not have another chance to see his nephew if he is as bad off as we believe.

The flight is long and uneventful, and my great-uncle is sullen and quiet. It will take him time to come to terms with all that is changing. When he retires to the master bedroom after dinner, it gives me time to review the documents Katarina put together and sent to my email. Every detail for the resort has been designed with customer input, and then I notice that while the footprint has been laid out, the detailed design for the inside and the operational flow still needs to be created.

There is a reference to an event pulling key stakeholders together to get that work done, and my excitement level goes up a notch or two. This could be just what I need to sink my teeth into. It's been the same old business dealings for some time now, nothing new or fresh, and I quickly scan through the rest of the articles.

She has managed to package everything Carlos always talked about into this plan, and as I flip to the next page, I'm surprised to see my name as operational owner paired beside hers as process owner. Katarina seems to be sincerely trying to do as my uncle has asked, and after reading through these documents and meeting her, she will have my full support. Unfortunately, our great-uncle will not be as easy to persuade.

I undress and get comfortable for the night on the pull-out sofa in the main cabin, and my mind drifts to Serena. I read the entire dossier on Serena and her family. She is twenty-four and went to airline attendant school just out of high school, where she graduated with honors. She worked for a commercial airline for two years and has been with the private firm we contract with for the last two. Her parents are deceased, but she has a grandmother still living, along with three older brothers who her grandmother practically raised.

She recently moved in with her nonna, and I skim the address in Naples, a middle-class zone, a relatively good part of town, while her brothers all live in the northern part of the country. Serena made monthly payments on her schooling, and it is paid in full. The home she lives in with her nonna is paid for, and I know that her medical bills are covered by our country's health plan. I scowl, trying to figure out what she intended to use the extra money she made from me for. Maybe medicine, because it looks like her nonna is in heart failure with the chronic obstructive pulmonary disease, but most of that should be covered, and with relatively few bills, her ratio of expense to salary is paltry, but there is literally nothing in her bank accounts. She has savings and checking, and both are well below one hundred dollars. It doesn't make any sense.

I text my guy to dig into her bank accounts and find out where the money is going. While Serena could undoubtedly be buying, she didn't look like a user, and that's the only other thing I can think of unless she has a gambling problem. I run my hands through my hair.

She just didn't seem the type, but I spend little to no time at all with a woman. A bit of socializing if it takes that to get them into bed, and even less if it's one of the girls from the club. They are the most willing and know precisely what I like and are always eager to please.

So why the hell am I sitting here searching her damn name on Facebook, trying to find a picture of her? I finally see her and click on the photo to enlarge it. Deep brown eyes, gorgeous silky dark hair, so thick and lush, and it's hanging down her shoulders, settled against the curvy outline of her breasts and those naturally colored red lips. Jesus, she is beautiful, and with all the women in the world that would do as I ask, she is the one that has somehow captured my full attention.

I send a message to Antonio, the security detail I had fly back home with Serena, to see how she is doing. She retired to the master bedroom for the night some time ago, and he believes she is doing fine, but the cameras are not on. "No, don't turn them on," I say, sharper than I intended in response to his question before disconnecting.

I save several pictures of her from Facebook and attach my favorite to her cell contact, hovering over it, contemplating calling her, but if her nonna is not well, she needs her sleep before she arrives. I am just about to fall asleep for the night myself when my cell buzzes.

Serena's nonna is being taken to the hospital by ambulance.

Get a crew on the ground to find out what happened. Serena doesn't know?

I don't know how she would.

Land in Naples, have a car waiting to take her to the hospital. In the meantime, get me the names and phone numbers of her brothers.

Consider it done.

Chapter 14

Serena

The ringing of my phone wakes me, and I squint at the bright sunlight coming into the jet's bedroom windows and reach for my phone, answering without looking at the caller. The husky voice at the other end sends an entirely unexplainable thrill through my body.

"I trust you slept well," Giovanni says as I glance at the time.

"It was amazing to sleep this long and in such comfort. Thank you so much for flying me back and allowing me to use this bedroom," I say.

"I'm glad you find my bed pleasing," he says, and just knowing that Gio has slept in this very room makes my cheeks heat with embarrassment and desire.

"I asked my security team to check on your nonna while you were in the air and she was taken to the hospital last night."

"What?" I cry, scrambling to sit upright and to understand what he's told me.

"I would have called you last night, but they learned that she was brought into the emergency room by ambulance and placed on a vent. She wasn't able to talk, Serena. I let you sleep, knowing that you would have worried all night and would have been unable to connect with her," Gio says.

"Oh, my God. How is she now? What happened?" I ask.

"Slow down. You know she has chronic obstructive pulmonary disease. She was admitted with respiratory acidosis. Basically, the carbon dioxide level in her blood went up so high that it caused the pH level in her blood to fall and her brain to lose its drive to breathe on her own. I checked on her this morning, and she's still in the ICU, and while critical, she's stable. The plane should land in about forty-five minutes. When you do, my driver will take you directly to the hospital, and you can join your brothers."

"Wait, my brothers are with her?"

"I had my team locate their phone numbers. I called them because you were in the air and arranged flights for them. They have been with your nonna since just after midnight," Gio says.

I am trying to process everything at once, and my body shivers with the unknown. "I don't know how I will ever thank you," I say.

"There's no need. You'll be landing soon. Take a nice hot shower and eat some breakfast. My guess is you won't have a lot of time once you get to the hospital."

I glance at the time and cringe. I'll have to hurry! "Okay, I'm going to do that. Thank you so much, Gio. I will never be able to repay you for your kindness, but know it means the world to me," I say, before disconnecting and heading to the bathroom.

* * *

When we land, a limo is waiting for us. Antonio opens the back door of the car for me and slides into the front passenger seat. The driver navigates through the bustling city, and when he stops I thank both him and Antonio for all of their help.

Antonio shakes his head with a smile. "Sorry, Serena. The boss wants me to stay with you, so you're stuck with me for a while," he says, opening my door to assist me out of the car and escorting me into the hospital.

"I don't know how to explain you to my brothers," I huff as we walk into the sterile-looking entrance and toward a long, sleek reception desk.

"I can be whoever you want me to be," Antonio says, laughing at his own joke.

The receptionist gives us directions to the ICU family waiting area. As the elevators open onto the upper floor my brothers are all there, Anzio, Aramis and Corino, and my heart constricts. It's only been four months since I've seen them, but it feels like forever. As soon as they see me, I am engulfed in large muscular arms. "How is she?" I ask.

My oldest brother, Anzio, speaks for everyone. "She isn't well, Serena. They had to put her on a vent before we arrived. It's going to be a waiting game for a while," he says.

I nod, just thankful that she didn't die, but saddened that she was alone while I was working again. Money! If only I had the funds to hire a full-time nurse to stay with her in our home or at least someone to sit with her. "Did she call the ambulance?" I ask, but my brothers all shake their heads, not knowing the answer to my question.

Antonio has been quiet but interjects. "I don't mean to intrude, but we learned last night that one of your neighbors went to see if she had some flour. I guess the lady was baking and ran out of what she needed. She found her passed out on the floor and called for help."

My middle brother, Aramis, looks at Antonio and then back to me. "I appreciate the information, but is someone going to tell us who this is and why the hell Giovanni Larussio personally called our homes and had us flown across the country in his private jet?" my brother asks, looking pointedly at me.

This is not good. The Larussio name is feared all over this land, and I can handle my brothers thinking Giovanni did this for me, but if this gets back to Nonna, it will absolutely kill her, and I will not allow it. "Such language," I admonish. "This is my boyfriend, Antonio, and he works for Giovanni. It was simply a favor to him," I say, taking in the shock registering in his eyes, and then his upturned lips as he smiles for my family.

Chapter 15

Katarina

I stir, rousing from a much-needed rest to a thrumming desire between my legs. I inhale and exhale, trying to keep my hunger at bay. If I touch myself, I will come, Chase will know, and the finale that he has planned for me will be diminished.

I reach over to the nightstand and pull up my laptop to check in on the Vegas project and busy my mind. The consultants are doing a fantastic job discovering the over-the-top amenities that people who frequent high-end resorts desire. I outline the items that align with my father's vision and will set the Larussio casino above the rest, and send a request to the general manager to have the architects include them for pricing. It is a couple hours later before I finish and head to the shower. I have just enough time to get ready for the evening before we touch down in LA.

I open the steel-and-black slate shower and smile. Even in the Carrington jet, Chase has thought to have all of my favorite brands of shampoo, conditioner, and body wash waiting for me. When I get out of the shower, I wrap myself in one of the towels from the warming station and select a smaller one for my hair. I put on my silver-and-diamond bracelets and matching necklace that I am seldom without, before applying a small amount of makeup. I unwrap my hair and towel dry the unruly mess before heading to the closet.

I stroke the material of the cobalt-blue dress in front of me, taking in the same-color strapless bra hanging in a lace bag beside it. The material feels silky and cool against the warmth of my skin, and I take a moment to look at my reflection in the mirror. The only adornment I have on my lower half is the long silver clit chain, and I know it will reach right above the hem of my dress, allowing Chase easy access throughout the night.

The dress smooths over my curves like it was made especially for me, because it probably was. It has an off-the-shoulder neckline, and the color emphasizes the blue of my eyes, and I step into a pair of pewter peep-styled boot heels that offset the style of the dress perfectly.

I have almost finished drying and straightening my hair into a glimmering shine when Chase walks into the bathroom. He lifts the long strands and pushes my hair aside, kissing my neck.

"You look absolutely amazing, Baby," he whispers in my ear while his hand slides up the side of my thigh, inching upward to grasp the chain.

He tugs gently on the chain and everything south clenches. Wearing the jewelry all afternoon has created a heated desire within me that is now just begging to be unleashed. He pulls my body back toward his, and I can feel his arousal, hard and erect, pushing against my bottom as he gently tugs again.

I moan softly. The pleasure building feels so good, and I know that it will be a very long evening while Chase increases my desire, stoking it hotter and hotter throughout the night. He gives the clit chain one more tug while his fingers caress along the smoothly waxed sides of my pussy before sliding my dress back in place and spinning me around to face him.

"I can't wait to introduce you to some of the more over-the-top stuff at the Carrington estates," he says, stepping away from me.

"Do tell," I say, kissing him gently on the lips.

"Patience, Baby, we'll get there," Chase says, smiling at me before heading to the bathroom to shower.

Gaby and I are talking in the main cabin when Chase comes out of the bedroom, dressed in a crisp white dress shirt with a custom-made black suit that shows his body to perfection.

He takes a seat beside us, and the pilot announces that we will be landing imminently. Once on the ground, the security team guides us from the private strip off of LAX to the awaiting helicopter. Chase stands behind me and scoops me into the copter to ensure no one has a view of what's underneath or what's not underneath my dress, before sliding in next to me.

"You're wicked," I whisper into his ear as he buckles me in.

"You haven't seen anything, yet, Baby," Chase says, smirking at me.

The flight isn't long, and we're soon touching down amid a backdrop of palm trees and majestic mountains. Brian Carrington's home is the epitome of a contemporary design owned by a person that controls a vast global steel empire. There is a lit pathway to what can only be considered a high-end Hollywood mansion. There are floors and floors made of steel and glass.

"Wow, this gives open concept an entirely new meaning," I say, taking it all in. You can see right into the home, and every floor has balconies with stairways leading to them, all encased in a steel structure.

"Indeed, I'm looking forward to seeing the lower level myself," Chase says, guiding me to the front door, where we are greeted by a friendly lady with blonde hair who opens the glass door.

"Welcome to the Carrington Estate. I'm Celia. Brian is expecting you, so I'll have your bags taken upstairs and take you to the lower level right away. Gaby, the kitchen is to the right. I'll just be a minute, and then we can visit for a little while," she says.

We walk through the foyer and are guided through a vast great room with black and white marble floors. The lights surrounding the estate are on, and it's easy to catch the views of swaying palms around a large outdoor pool as we make our way through the glass-walled home.

We follow her to an elevator, and Jay and Sheldon are both texting on their phones, no doubt making sure the facility is secured to their liking. The doors open and we walk through the lounge toward an expansive bar. Above us are gilded cages hanging from the ceiling, and nude women except for heels and thongs are swaying to the erotic music that is gently pulsing through the room. Chase guides me through the club, navigating around the tables set up throughout the room. We reach the bar and Chase lifts me, setting me onto one of the barstools.

"I'm Brett, what would you like to drink?" the man behind the bar asks.

"Baby?" Chase asks.

"Hmm. I think I'll take water for now," I say, still recovering from last night and all the cranberry vodkas I drank.

"One water and a Dalmore for me," Chase says.

"Sure thing, coming right up," the bartender says, placing our drinks in front of us before moving on to another customer at the end of the bar.

My eyes are drawn to the monitors mounted over the bar. There are people in various degrees of dress partaking in various sexual acts all on display overhead.

One woman is being handcuffed to a bed with an ornate headboard. She is spread wide while her partner uses his fingers to allow the group an in-depth look at her wetness. She raises her hips, turned-on by the fact people are watching her.

On another monitor, a long-haired blonde is stretched over a spanking bench. Her black lacy panties are pooled at the bottom of her four-inch spiky red heels. Her thighs are lily white, and her ass is well-toned and round, on display for all to see what her partner intends to do. He walks around to her front and affixes her wrists with handcuffs, rendering her captured, before whispering something in her ear.

He walks toward a wall in the room which is adorned with floggers and an assortment of whips and canes, appraising each of them before selecting his implement. He raises it and lets the strands touch and caress her, bringing out the sensitivity and her desire. I see her hips and ass rise in the air and only then does he begin little flicks of the implement, starting slow and then increasingly letting it rain down on her shoulders, her back, and buttocks, bringing the blood to the surface and fueling her desire.

When she raises her hips, he delivers a more intense pattern, leaving crisscrosses of heat on her lily white skin. She begins moaning with evident pleasure, and I feel myself moistening to the point that I need to look away.

I try to focus on my drink, but the magnetism of Chase's deep green eyes watching me draws me to look at him. "Watch the other rooms, Baby," he says, leaning down to kiss my lips softly.

The one that captures my attention is the woman tied to the St. Andrew's Cross. She is nude except for five-inch purple platform heels. Her hands are secured above her to the cross. The man is fully dressed in black dress pants and a black sweater and is working to restrain her middle to the cross, and then her ankles. The man circles her as if about ready to devour her before whispering something in her ear. She keens, entirely at his mercy.

The moan from another screen catches my attention. A long-haired blonde is lying prone on the bed, hands restrained overhead and ankles cuffed to the polished metal of the footboard. The man is kissing down her body and slows as he reaches her mons. She tries to rise, but he doesn't allow it. It's clear he wants complete and absolute control of her pleasure, and just the thought alone makes me wet with anticipation.

I feel the heat of Chase's eyes on me and then the slow and steady thrum of the clit chain turning on. I am on fire, ready to explode, and I squirm in my chair just before he turns the suction off, causing me to squeeze my legs together, frustrated with unleashed desire, but thankful he did not make me climax in a room full of people.

His hand glides against the small of my back, pulling me closer. "I think you're ready for what I have in store for you now," Chase says, assisting me from the barstool.

Chapter 16

Chase

"I hope I chose well," I say, guiding her down the hall until we reach the room I have selected. I open the door, turn on the lights, and push the button that brings the blinds down over the glass window. "No prying eyes, from the hall or overhead. I am not sharing you with anyone," I say, pushing another button that is labeled with the word camera.

"Oh my God, Chase. It's unbelievable," Katarina says, looking around the room. There is an ornate pewter four-poster bed situated against the middle of the far wall that has restraints hanging from each corner. On the far side of the room sits a spanking bench custom designed with the Carrington Steel logo. It is made of sturdy grey steel with a long plum-colored pad that you can lay someone across, and matching knee cushions to ensure comfort and maximum visibility.

She swallows, unsure what I intend for her this evening. Her eyes are focused on the wall adorned with a variety of floggers, whips, and belts, but it is the paddle section that holds her attention. Wooden paddles, all in a variety of shapes and sizes. Then there are silver-handled paddles with rubber ends.

I watch her as she walks along the wall, taking in the assortment of toys. Her eyes then settle with interest on the floor-to-ceiling-mirrored corner of the room. An extended apparatus hangs from a track in the ceiling. There are multiple cords attached to one another with black rubber objects affixed.

"It's a swing, Baby. I thought you might like to go for a little ride tonight," I say, lifting her hair and caressing the sensitive skin of her neck with my tongue while sliding the zipper down her back. The smooth material wafts to the floor and pools around her legs, leaving her in the lacy blue strapless bra, pewter high-heeled boots, and her silver-and-diamond jewelry. I know her body has been thrumming with anticipation all afternoon, and that she is more than ready.

"Lift your hair for me, Baby," I say, scooping the mass of long auburn curls and unclasping the fastener on her necklace that releases the chain to its full length, exposing the silver and diamond nipple clamps for what they are. I turn her to face me, and the passion reflected in her blue eyes burns through me.

"I think you're a bit overdressed," I say, releasing the clip that allows the small weight of her breasts to bounce as she is freed from the silky material. I pull her close, capturing her sensual lips, and she parts for me and begins to shiver as I move the chain in little circles, stimulating and teasing her. When I lift her, Katarina's legs instinctively go around my waist, and her arms tighten around my neck until I have her comfortably placed into the black rubber seat of the swing.

"Don't let go until I have you safely harnessed," I say, taking one of her wrists and placing it on the cord over her head, and then the other, then positioning her heels, one at a time, into the restraints on either side of my waist. She is nestled in the swing, her arms raised above her head and legs spread apart to allow me to stand between them.

Her eyes are heated with desire and anticipation, and I know in this position she feels exposed. I take time just to admire my beautiful wife waiting for me to pleasure her. I reach overhead and give the pulley a tug to bring the rubber support down lower, making sure her neck is cradled within it before undressing.

My cock throbs as I rub it against her silky center, brushing against the chain affixed to her clit as I caress and the suck her nipples. When I run the silver-and-diamond side of the necklace against the sensitive tips, she moans with pleasure.

"So beautiful, Baby, let me hear you," I say, squeezing one of her nipples before affixing the diamond-ringed nipple clamp. It closes around her skin, and she inhales deeply, absorbing the exquisite pain and resounding pleasure that it brings. I lick the tip of her nipple as she adjusts to its restraint, and then move to the other side, paying just as much attention to it before adhering the second clamp.

"Baby, I want to see you, all of you," I say, spreading the pulleys wide, slowly exposing her even further to my gaze, adjusting her so I can lower her hands and tilt her backward. Her neck is cradled in the black rubber headrest, and she is suspended in the air with her legs spread as far as they can possibly go, and the movement has created a pull of the chain on her nipples. She licks her lips and tilts her head sideways, trying to absorb the pleasure.

My finger runs the length of her, center to front, circling her captive clit, tugging gently on the dangling necklace affixed to her erect and pulsing tips. She moans, and the sound goes directly to my cock, and it hardens to stone.

I use the pulleys to glide her upward until my face is level with her center. "So beautiful, Baby," I say, caressing her folds with the heat of my tongue, gently teasing around the clit chain. Katarina is close, but this will not be over quickly, because pushing her boundaries and pleasuring her is an addiction for me.

I caress her softly with my tongue, exploring, and then start the clit chain. The vibrations start, and she tenses, but in this position is left unable to push into the sensations or away from them. She moans with pleasure, and I tug gently on her nipple chain. It sends her crashing over the edge, wave after wave, and she cries out my name over and over, until I slow the pulsation and then eventually turn it to off and allow her to come down from her orgasm, breathless and panting.

"Baby, so responsive. Are you ready to go for a little ride?" I ask, adjusting the swing and pushing my cock deep inside of her with one thrust forward.

She moans as I seat myself deep and begin gliding the swing slightly, holding her hips, guiding her back so that my cock pulls out holding her right on edge. I bring her forward, and the motion of the swing causes her to glide onto my cock, and it drives deep, causing her to moan with pleasure as I do it time and time again. "I can't take it anymore," she says, panting at the same time her head tilts back trying to absorb the pleasure.

"You know your safeword, Baby, and I haven't heard it yet," I say, swinging her out once more. This time when I swing her onto my cock, the penetration causes her to cry out bringing us both over the edge as I thrust through the waves until we are both entirely spent.

She lays her head back against the cradle of the swing, still breathless, as I work to remove her restraints and carry her to the bed, cradling her in my arms while our breathing slowly returns to normal. Her eyes are still hazy half an hour later while she watches me clean between her thighs. "So good," she says, smiling up at me.

"I'm glad you were pleased, Mrs. Prestian. Are you ready to join our friends, or would you rather stay here for a while?" I ask, pushing her auburn curls from her face.

"We can go find Jenny and Brian if I can still walk," she says, lifting herself out of my arms. I swat her ass playfully and watch as she makes her way across the room.

When Katarina walks back in from the bathroom, she looks hotter than any runway model I've ever seen. "If I didn't tell you earlier, that dress looks amazing on you," I say.

"Thank you," she says, almost shyly. "What are you doing, working?" Katarina asks, gesturing with a nod of her head to where I have just finished typing an entry into my phone.

I smirk. "No, I was ordering a swing," I reply, watching Katarina's eyes light up and her cheeks pink as she swipes a bit of coral color onto her lips.

She smiles widely. "You liked that as much as I did?" she asks, walking toward me and curling onto my lap.

"I enjoyed it immensely, Katarina. You never cease to amaze me, Baby," I say, standing with her and capturing her lips.

"I need to rinse off in the shower. While I'm doing that, write down your ten favorite toys in this room. I'm looking forward to seeing what you select," I say, kissing Katarina deeply before heading to the shower where I think about all the possibilities of her continued journey.

It's later in the evening when Brian gets called down to the lower level in response to an altercation occurring in one of the entertainment rooms. Jay and I accompany him downstairs, and they head into one of the back rooms while I talk with some of our security team who has congregated across the room.

I cringe as Katarina and Jenny walk back into the club and I see what's captured their attention on the overhead monitors. Sasha, Brian's ex, is lying on a bed, completely nude, facing the camera, and Brian is rubbing lotion all over her back. Jenny heads straight to the bar so she can watch the scene play out, while Katarina searches me out and is by my side in moments, fuming mad.

"It's not what you think, Baby. He's not cheating on Jenny. Sasha was with someone that was hurting her, and Brian and Jay had to intervene. Jay was with him until just a few minutes ago, and he's probably just applying a numbing cream. I sent him a text to let him know the cameras are still on, but he hasn't read it," I say.

"Hurt her how?" Katarina asks.

"The guy she partnered with kept hitting her with a whip. He must have been on something or didn't know what he was doing. Regardless, he didn't stop when she safeworded."

"That's awful, but it's about to get worse. Jenny's heading back there right now," Katarina says, and I watch as her best friend slides off the barstool and heads down the hall just as Jay walks up to us.

"What the fuck is that camera still on for, and what the fuck is Brian doing?" Jay spews, talking to no one in particular and not waiting for an answer as he stalks past us, making his way back down the hall. So much for my calm-and-collected head of security. I've never seen him so worked up. He's in the room for all of two seconds before the show on the overhead disappears, replaced by a black monitor.

"Okay, and what was that all about? Jay has never come unglued like that before," Katarina says.

"I'm as puzzled as you are right now," I say, guiding her back to the rest of my security team, who have grown in numbers and seem unusually animated.

They stop talking as we approach. "The man has been taken care of?" I ask.

"Umm, yeah, Jay took care of things himself," Sheldon says, glancing at Katarina and then me, seemingly ill at ease. He and I get a message at the same time and glance at our phones.

"Change of plan men," I say to the team. "Matt has been working to uncover some information in Chicago. Brian and I received a call a short time ago alerting us to the fact that he may be in trouble. Jay has teams mobilized, and they are working to locate Matt as we speak. In the meantime, he's going to be sending each of you a reassignment. Sheldon, he's asking that you run the point for both Katarina and myself in Italy. He's sending another team in to support you, as he won't be making the trip. He's staying back in the States, taking the young lady that was hurt tonight and Brian's house manager, Celia, to Brian's condo across town. He plans to stay with them tonight and then leave for Chicago to help the team get Matt tomorrow. He'll have it all communicated and arranged later tonight, but that's the high-level summary," I say.

The team is solemn, knowing one of their own could be in trouble. "Sounds good, Chase. I'll let the other men know when they get back," Sheldon says.

I raise my eyebrows. "Get back from where?"

"A bit of a mess with the man that hurt the blonde. Nothing you need or should know about. It's being dealt with, and I'll relay the info they need when they get back," Sheldon says.

I nod, knowing that some things are just better left not discussed. "Very well. Thanks for all of your help tonight. We'll see some of you in the morning," I say, guiding my exhausted wife to our bedroom.

* * *

I'm working on my laptop when the alarm goes off at 3:00 a.m. Katarina wakes slowly and stretches. I put the notebook aside, pull her into my lap, and push her unruly curls to the side so that I can nuzzle her creamy neck. She leans into me and presses against the hardness of my cock pulsing underneath her bottom.

"Good morning. As much as I would love to stay in bed for just a few more minutes, we need to be up in the air shortly. Your clothes are on the chair, and toothpaste and toothbrush are on the counter for you. We can shower on the plane later in the day," I say.

She groans with pouty reluctance. "Go now, we'll play on the plane. Jay has jets scrambled, and we need to be on the one heading out of the Carrington private strip in less than thirty minutes."

She slips off my lap, careful to press her bottom into my throbbing cock, and puts a little swing in her hips as she grabs her clothes and walks to the bathroom. I smirk as she openly teases me. She's sure to get a punishment we'll both enjoy.

When she returns, I'm dressed and ready to go, texting Sheldon that we're on the move. When we arrive on the first floor, Sheldon and Dereck meet us, escorting us to the awaiting limo. I slide in next to Katarina in the center of the limo. Sheldon and Dereck close the doors and climb into the back before I hit the button that engages the privacy glass and renders our conversation private. I pull Katarina against me, laying her head in my lap, knowing she is not a morning person and that she needs way more sleep than the few hours we've gotten. "Sleep Baby," I say, running my hands through her hair, but instead, she nuzzles her face against my cock, instantly rewarded with a hardened member.

She rubs the warmth of her mouth over my cock and unzips me, using one finger to slide underneath my underwear so that she can kiss and lick my head. I hear my own breath catch, as she takes the crown into her mouth, exploring my slit with her tongue. I grasp her hair harder, but let her keep control of the reins. The power of providing pleasure is heady, and she moans as she slides my length all the way to the back of her throat.

"Baby," I moan as her lips glide up and down my length, sucking me, while her hands slide under me to cup my balls. She feels them tighten and pushes against that spot I love, and I groan with pleasure. She knows that I am close and uses her tongue to tease me further, gliding up and down while sucking even harder.

"We're pulling into the strip," Sheldon says overhead.

She lifts her head like that's the end, but I don't think so. My hand on her hair tightens. The climax is building and is on its way, and she takes me in deep, sucking hard and flattening her tongue against my cock. My breath is harsh and ragged, and my hand in her hair urges her up and down over my cock, right before I send a load of come into her mouth. She sucks and licks, cleaning me quickly, zipping me before glancing up in a panic at being caught.

I pull her into my lap to face me before I hit another button on the door.

"What is that button for," Katarina says when the privacy glass does not come up.

I smile at her and give her a kiss. "It lets them know that we're busy, Baby," I say.

She narrows her bright blue eyes at me. "You don't think I would ever let our team walk in on us, or open the door when you're in a compromised position, do you?" I say.

"I should have known better," Katarina says.

"But you were turned on by the possibility of getting caught?" I ask, kissing her lips.

She shakes her head, and I narrow my eyes at her, letting her know that I want the truth. "I can't deny that it did turn me on," Katarina says.

“I like that very much, Baby,” I say right before Sheldon opens the car door.

“Plane’s ready, and the flights have all been scrambled. If everything goes as planned, they won’t be watching this plane but will have eyes on the Prestian Corp plane traveling from New York to Italy. Either way, we should probably get in the air,” Sheldon says.

Chapter 17

Gio

I'm just reading the text that lets me know Serena is with her brothers and nonna at the hospital. They are not allowing anyone in at the moment due to an infectious ailment in the community and her breathing capabilities. One infection could kill her, so the family is left to wait. I ask Antonio for a play-by-play, and he checks in every half hour, but nothing seems to change, just more waiting.

I'm texting Antonio when my great-uncle walks in. "Your little assistant seems to be keeping you busy. Flights registered for her family all over the country, our intel running background checks on her and her family," he says, settling into the recliner in preparation for our landing.

I shrug. "You asked for a background check, no?" I say.

"And the family flights? She hasn't been cleared yet, Giovanni. You have Antonio out in the field with her and her family," he says, leveling his dark eyes at me.

"He's fine and has been giving me periodic updates," I say.

"So I hear. Get the young lady cleared or stay away from her, Giovanni," he says as the plane's wheels hit the ground.

I know the rules, and damn if I haven't broken every one of them letting her anywhere near the family, our security team, giving her my personal cell number. I knew when I did it that having her family board the private family jet without clearance would be cause for our team to alert him. The thought of her dealing with her grandmother alone was just too much though. "I understand. It will be done soon."

I send a note to intel to work faster to get her background done and clear her through the level one security reserved only for people that you intend to have in your residence, personal cars, etc. The women you go and see at clubs are secured with a far lesser grade, and although security is tight, nothing like a level one.

We reach the awaiting limo and get in, and he is intently reading the message on his phone but turns his hard gaze to me. "A level one, Giovanni?"

I knew they would alert him and am prepared. "I'm considering Serena for a full-time personal assistant position. I decided to take your advice and get more help," I say.

He raises his eyes from the message he's reading on the phone. "Be very careful, Giovanni, the family rules are in place for a reason," he says.

I don't like that comment one little bit, especially coming from the don of the Italian Family, and vow to get her cleared as quickly as possible, but level one will take a bit of time.

* * *

I work from my home office for the next two days and am dealing with a situation that will take me out of town, which means the meeting scheduled with Katarina and Chase will need to be moved. It's unavoidable. I'm going to need to be there in person to deal with this, and my uncle loves to visit Paris. I give him a call to let him know the flight details and am pleasantly surprised that he accepts right away and I don't need to talk him into it. I have just hung up with him when a message from Antonio comes through.

Serena is leaving later today. Going to the U.S. Flight turns straight around and comes back. A Prestian Corp jet needs a flight crew last minute notice. She's accepted the job.

I haven't contacted her once. As much as I wanted to text her, I wanted to give her the space she needed with her family. She was in such a rush to get back to her nonna, even when she just thought she wasn't feeling well. Now she's in the hospital, and she's just going to leave her? She hasn't even gotten to see her yet. What the hell is she thinking?

I gather my briefcase and bag and text my driver to meet me out front and to have the plane ready on the private strip for my uncle and me. I need to be in Paris and will deal with her in the air. I get to the jet, talk to the pilot and crew for a moment before my uncle joins us, surrounded by security, until we are settled in the plane. He immediately heads to the back bedroom, telling me he has work to do, but I see his weariness. I settle into the main cabin and connect with her number. "Hold on, let me get to better reception," Serena says, and I wait with growing impatience until she returns to the line. "I'm back, Gio. Thanks for calling," Serena says.

"Antonio tells me you accepted a job to go to America with Prestian Corp. How is it that you wish to leave your nonna without seeing her?" I ask.

"It's nothing I have control over. I need the money, not that I would expect you to know anything about that," Serena says.

"Money for what? What do you spend your paycheck on? Your nonna's house is paid for, her health care is paid for, you use public transportation and make a good wage. Tell me what you're doing with it, Serena?" I say.

"How do you know this, Giovanni Larussio? Tell me!"

I smile broadly. This woman dares sass me, but her little tirade is far from over.

"I don't expect you to understand anything about a family that has no money, and that money is the only thing that will keep Nonna alive and comfortable in her last days," Serena says, and I hear the muffled sob just before the line goes quiet.

She's fucking muted me, and something just isn't adding up. Right now I would love to just fuck Paris and fly instead to Naples, and spank the truth out of this dark-haired beauty, but instead, I wait.

It's a brief pause before she comes back on the line. "Sorry, must be a bad connection. I appreciate your concern, but I need to do this," Serena says.

We'll discuss her deceit later while she's lying over my thighs with her ass presented to me for a sound spanking. "Who will be with your nonna?" I ask.

"Aramis has to get back to work, but my other brothers can stay and work remotely. It won't be a long assignment, pretty much fly to America and then right back. It pays too much to turn down," Serena says, and my jaw clenches. Three goddamn brothers that, from what my intel has uncovered, all make much more than her, and she's doing whatever she can to scrape together money for her and her nonna. What the hell kind of family is it that they don't take care of her, make sure Serena can be with her grandmother in her last days?

The need to take care of her is entirely unfamiliar, nothing I've ever felt for a woman. "Serena, there's no need to take the assignment. I'll cover whatever it is that you need. Stay, be with your nonna in case she wakes," I say and then she starts to cry.

"It's very kind, and I don't know how to thank you for everything, but the simple truth is that I can't take money from you. I'm sorry, Gio. Please don't take it personally," Serena says, softly sobbing, disconnecting and leaving me once again on the empty line of a telephone call.

Now, all I want to do is turn her curvy bare ass over my knee and spank her until she tells me what I want to know and agrees to my terms, but instead I call Antonio in frustration, who answers in one ring. "Yeah, boss," he says.

"What the hell is going on? Did Serena or her family give you any clue why she would leave now? She hasn't even had a chance to be with her grandmother," I say.

"Hang on," Antonio says, and I scowl at having to wait again. He comes back on the line in a few moments. "So the reception is okay in the waiting area. I just needed some privacy. Same reason Serena stepped out when you called. She doesn't want her family to think that you're involved with her in any way."

"How the fuck do you know that?" I ask.

"When I first got here, her brothers were giving her heat, asking why you were calling them and offering flights. She gave them some bullshit story. It was clear that she didn't want them to think she had anything to do with you."

I hear what he's saying, and I completely understand why she would feel that way, but the more I process it, the harder I want to pound something. Time and time again, it comes back to this. My fucking heritage! The one I've tried to get out from under all of my life, the very one that she is not in the slightest willing to embrace, and if I'm honest, the one that I would warn her to stay far, far away from if I instead didn't want her in my arms and in my bed.

"Take her to the airstrip, make sure she is on board and settled in with the Prestian Corp security before you leave her. If she's taking off in a couple hours, it's too late to get you on that plane.

They would demand a clearance of their own. In the interim, run her credit card and any expenses she pays for during her travel, Antonio. I want to know everything she does, and keep me apprised of her grandmother's condition," I say.

"Yeah, boss. Gotta go, have a little situation here," Antonio says before disconnecting and leaving me with no clue what the fuck is going on.

Chapter 18

Serena

I return to the reception area, and my brothers are talking in raised voices, animated amongst themselves, but they quiet as I enter the room.

Anzio, the oldest, is the first to speak. "The Mafiosi just showed up at my family's door. My wife had to answer that door, fearing for her life and that of our children. You tell me what the fuck is going on, right now, Serena!" Anzio yells.

My worst nightmare, the one where my family is pulled into my reality is coming true, but there is no possibility that I can let them know what happened, give Nonna's secret away. I swore that I would not tell anyone in my family and I won't.

I push hard against my brother's firm chest. "Stop it! You think I would knowingly bring the Family down on your family's doorstep. Just stop, I would never," I cry before he picks me up and sets me down on the couch in the waiting room, occupied by only our family.

"You need to tell us what's going on, the truth," Anzio says, his hard dark brown eyes flashing with gold bits of passion as he chastises me.

I swore I wouldn't, but as soon as I missed a payment, even though I told them why, they went after my brother and his family. This is what I was afraid of, and now, not only is my nonna in danger but my brothers and their families, too. As long as I kept making the payments, my family was safe.

If I tell them the truth, they will go head-to-head with the Mafiosi. I know my headstrong siblings, and I will not put them in any more danger than they are already in.

"I owe them money. I had to cut my last trip short and didn't have enough to make the full payment. I've accepted a job to America and back. Once I return, I'll be able to make my payment," I say.

"What did you do, Serena? How did you become indebted to them?" Corino asks.

"Many ways, dear brother. Let's not talk about it today. Instead, let's ensure that we have a plan to take care of Nonna and that one of us is with her when she wakes. I would hate it if she woke up from this scared and alone," I say.

"She won't be leaving the hospital for some time, based on the doctor's report. She will be well cared for. We're going underground with our families until this is taken care of. You need to come with us."

"No, thanks. Just make sure your families are safeguarded. When I return, I'll have enough to make this month's payment and next month's," I say, but none of them are listening.

Anzio points to Antonio. "You keep her safe, or I'll come for you," he says as they all walk right out of the room, turning their backs on me. The tears fall, and Antonio walks toward me.

"We should leave if you want to catch that flight. I'll take you to the airstrip," Antonio says gently.

I nod, grabbing my purse and sweater, my heart aching with the weight of everything that is happening as we walk to the awaiting limo. “I don’t know how to thank you,” I say as the driver pulls away, and we wind through the city until we reach the countryside and turn into the drive that takes us to the private airstrip.

“No need. I’ll walk you up, but then they’ll have their own security. You’ll be perfectly safe until you return. I’ll meet you when you land,” Antonio says, opening the door of the limo and escorting me up the ramp to the Prestian Corp jet.

Chapter 19

Katarina

"The security teams don't even require me in restraints," I whisper to Chase across the table after looking around to ensure no one else is listening to our conversation.

Chase smiles. "But we both know how much I love holding you captive, Baby," he says.

"All this time, you've been securing me with these things on all of our private trips, just like on the commercial planes, and it wasn't necessary," I say, pretending to be upset.

"You know how much your safety means to me, Katarina. The private plane rules were created for people that don't take safety that seriously, and they don't apply to my wife. You will always be buckled in, secured, to make sure you are protected in takeoff and landing. Does that bother you?" Chase asks, pushing my unruly curls behind my ears.

I shake my head. "I know you want me to be safe, and I was really just teasing you," I say, playfully.

"Teasing me about your safety?" Chase asks, his deep green

eyes raising at my comment as the jet taxis down the runway and lifts into the air.

He does not joke about my security, and he's made that entirely clear from the start of our relationship. As hard as it's been for me to adapt to a life with security guards following my every move, they have saved my life and his on more occasions then I can count, and I wouldn't want it any other way now.

"Maybe I wanted to get spanked for such blatant disregard for my safety," I say.

His eyes flash with delight. "Careful what you wish for, Baby. You know that can be easily accommodated. Unbuckle and come sit on my lap," he says once we're in the air.

I slip out of my seat, and he leans back in his chair, gesturing for me to spin around and face the other way. I look around the cabin, knowing he has pushed a privacy button that will ensure no one walks in on us. He pulls me down in his lap, and I can feel the strength of his chest against my back, and the hardness of his erection underneath me.

"Did you like the spanking benches you saw at Brian's?" Chase asks, the warmth of his breath in my ear sending goosebumps down my arms.

I nod. Chase will always want to talk about our sexual experiences, what I liked, what I didn't, and what my hidden desires might be. He's been open and honest about that from the start of our relationship, and I know that pleasing me is essential to him. His need is to understand my darkest desires and to let me explore them.

"I loved the entire lower level, and I can't stop thinking about what you did to me there."

"I'm glad you liked the experience, and if you'd like to return, I'm more than happy to take you back. In fact, that was the exact reaction I was hoping for," Chase says.

"Do I have to wait to get spanked there?" I ask.

"Baby, you know better than that. Consequences are best delivered as soon as the transgression occurs," Chase says, taking my hand in his and rubbing small circles into my palm with his index finger. "Besides, we have hours and hours in the air," he says.

I know what he's doing, creating the same pattern that he uses when caressing my clit with his tongue, and I'm unable to stem the moistness gathering between my legs as he strokes my hand and kisses the sensitive skin of my nape, causing me to shiver with desire.

"Spread your legs for me," Chase whispers.

My thighs open and his fingers leave my palm and slide my skirt up. He rubs my mound through my panties, and when I think I can't possibly stand it anymore, he slides his finger under the lacy material, grazing my aroused clit with his touch. He caresses me, finding that particular spot, stroking me until I moan. My hips raise of their own accord, but his other hand pushes my lower belly down, holding me in place. I am right on edge, and he does not stop, his finger gliding across my aching clit. He caresses the sensitive skin of my earlobe and uses his tongue to explore my ear. I moan with pleasure and raise up, but he holds me in place, rubbing me. "Now, come for me, Katarina," Chase whispers, and I do, shaking uncontrollably against his magic finger and the hardness of his body.

He holds me tight as the aftershocks start to recede. I feel his cock, hard and erect, throbbing against me. "I think I earned dessert, Baby," Chase says capturing my waist and settling me on the table in front of us to face him. My skirt has fallen past my waist again, covering me, and he lifts it. "Hold it up so I can see you," he whispers.

I do as he asks, raising it above my legs.

"Your panties are all wet. I think we need to get rid of them.

Raise your ass for me, or I'll be forced to rip them off of you," Chase says.

I lift up, and he navigates my panties down my legs and off my body. He slides them in front of his nose and inhales deeply.

"I'll never get tired of the scent of your arousal," Chase says, pocketing my panties in his suit jacket before pushing me down onto the table and spreading my legs in front of him. "I was going to order cheese and crackers and a little wine when we boarded, but I much prefer this dessert," Chase says, his deep green eyes watching me intently as he lets his tongue slide over the most sensitive part of my body. He is slow, in no hurry, and his eyes never leave mine. I am the first to look away because as the pleasure grasps me, I want something to hold on to as the waves overtake me. I run my hands through his hair, tightening my grip as he brings me right to the edge, but then changes patterns.

He pulls one of our toys out of his pocket and shows it to me before he brings it to my lips. "Suck Baby."

I take the glass-like object into my mouth, sucking it deep into my throat, lubricating it with my saliva, and my tongue.

"Enough," Chase says, pulling the overly generous dildo from my lips and sliding it into my slick center. He pushes it deep inside of me, and I moan with pleasure as he finds a pattern that keeps hitting that sensitive spot at the very back of my core, before he takes it out and runs it between the cheeks of my ass. "I want to feel this, stroking you inside, right alongside my cock," he says, slowly inserting it into my bottom hole.

"Chase," I moan, attempting to acclimate to the exquisite feel of the dildo and his tongue as he takes me into his mouth, encircling my clit at the same time he inserts two fingers deep inside of me. They move in and out, curling. They are both rubbing against that spot. I moan, and he moves from my clit to my lips, capturing the sound with his mouth, exploring my tongue with his own before pulling his fingers out and sinking his cock deep inside of me. It is hard and rigid, and the fullness from both him and the vibrations of the plug are intense. He thrusts deeply, in perfect rhythm with the vibration of the plug, causing me to cry out, repeating his name time and time again as the waves of ecstasy overtake me, until he releases deep inside of me, pulling me close and cradling me as our bodies recover.

He is the first to move, kissing me on the lips as I slowly come back to earth. "You're tired, Baby, let me get you washed up and into bed," Chase says, pulling out of me and removing the toy from my bottom to take into the bathroom.

He returns with a washcloth and towel. "Spread your legs for me, Baby," Chase says, and he washes me with the warm cloth, tracing where he's been, moving it gently through my folds. While I used to be embarrassed being this exposed and open to him, I now find the aftercare and intimacy we share just as much a part of the pleasure as the act itself.

When he's done washing me, he kisses me on the lips. "Let's get you to bed. You haven't had much for sleep, and it's going to be a long flight," he says, placing his hand behind my knees, lifting me. My hands automatically wrap around his neck as he carries me still nude into our master suite and settles me on the bed, before pulling the lightweight down comforter over me.

"Sleep Baby, I have some work that I need to do," Chase says, kissing my lips before sliding into a pair of lounge pants and a t-shirt and heading back into the main cabin while I snuggle into the warmth of the down comforter.

It is hours later when I wake and stretch, feeling as though I have finally caught up with my sleep. The last few weeks have been troubling, worried about my parents and how they are doing after the accident, Kate's charges, and all the court proceedings. Now I have to deal with my very real great-uncle who acts like he wants to welcome me into the folds of the Italian Family while intending to intervene with my father's legacy.

I slide out of bed to freshen up and then start rummaging through the closet. I'm not surprised to find several outfits that are all similar in style to what I wore for my initial meeting with my great-uncle. A short skirt, sexy, strappy shoes, the higher the heel, the better.

I skim through the options that Chase has had placed in my closet and shake my head. I don't know how he does it, or his shopper does, but they hit the nail on the head every single time. I skim the closet and know that when we go to meet my uncle on his own ground, I will be slipping into the short black skirt, the red lace cami, and matching the black jacket. The heels are signature classic black five-inch heels with a red platform, sending the same message as before, red, black and white, Vegas colors that send a symbolic message of their own. Whoever picked this outfit for me was spot-on, and that helps offset some of the anxiety about meeting the entire family when we're in Italy.

Chapter 20

Chase

A couple hours later, I'm buried in the MacBook in front of me and glance up as Katarina walks into the main cabin, taking her in from head to toe. "You look stunning, Baby," I say, admiring the pretty yellow dress and gesturing for her to sit on my lap. I wrap my arms around her warmth, kissing the top of her hair and pushing a wayward strand from her lovely face. It's at moments like this that I wonder how I've been so lucky to have found her.

"Sleep well?" I ask.

"Um, huh," she says, tilting her lips for a kiss.

Sheldon walks in and looks sheepish. "Sorry guys, the privacy light wasn't on, and the door was unlocked," he says.

"It's fine, Sheldon. Katarina just woke up. What's on your mind," I say, holding Katarina steady as she starts to squirm to get off my lap. I smirk. She's so cute when her cheeks flush with embarrassment.

He looks pointedly at Katarina and then back at me. While I'd prefer to keep her from worry, she senses something is amiss.

"Speak freely, Sheldon," I say, earning a small smile. This is her family, and she has a right to know what's happening.

"Our teams spotted boats just off the coast of Italy, pretty sure they're keeping tabs on your house right now, Chase. I've been briefed on the security system and guard perimeter around the property. The men haven't seen anything except the boats. We've got intel running searches, but we're pretty sure we'll run into dummy registrations, and I think we both know who it is," Sheldon says.

I know exactly who it is and am not surprised in the least. "Not to worry, Sheldon. When Katarina and I arrive home, we'll let him know we're in Italy and are planning to spend some time with my family before we meet with him and the rest of Katarina's family."

"So after the effort we've gone through to ensure they didn't know when you were arriving, you're just going to announce that you're in Italy," Sheldon asks.

"It will make for a great icebreaker," I say, smirking at the smile on his face.

"I can't wait to see how this shit goes down," Sheldon says, grinning.

I laugh. "You'll have a front-row seat, still running point, right?" I say.

Sheldon nods. "Roger that, as soon I get a game plan together," he says, shaking his head before disappearing back into the security quarters behind the flight crew.

The door opens again, and this time Katarina wiggles off my lap to sit across the table from me as our lunch is served. The rest of the afternoon is spent working side by side while Katarina completes the outline for the final touches on the Vegas deal and I develop a proposal to purchase another small healthcare facility. She's copied both me and Giovanni Larussio on the work she's done. I read it, fascinated by her intelligence and attention to detail.

She closes her MacBook, stands, and stretches.

"This is really good, Katarina." I can't think of one question I have that wasn't answered in her brief. "It will make the attorney's job much easier, especially if we get pushback from the family," I say.

"You think we will? I don't quite have a handle on Giovanni yet. I've sent him several emails, trying to keep him informed, and he hasn't responded at all," Katarina says.

"Time will tell. Why don't we give your dad a call?"

"That would be great! I'd love to run some of the future state proposals by him, just to see what he thinks," Katarina says, her eyes dancing with excitement.

"I'll have our teams scramble the communication trail to make sure no one is listening, it'll just take a minute or two," I say, dialing her parents' number through the security line and placing it on speaker. We can hear the clicks in the background, redirecting the lines.

The phone finally quits clicking and her mother answers.

"Hi, Mom," Katarina says.

"Sweetie, it's so good to hear your voice. Are you in Italy?" she asks.

"Not yet, almost. I was hoping to give Dad an update on the Vegas expansion if he's awake and feeling up to it."

"I feel fine," her father bellows from the background, and Katarina smiles widely.

"You sure sound a lot better. Getting stronger and faster every day I hear," Katarina says, teasing him.

"Haven't felt this good in a long time. We're going to take a walk in the woods later today. I've been cooped up too damn long.

Everything's healing nicely, I just need to keep working to get my muscle strength back," Carlos says.

"Well if you're feeling that good, maybe you can help me make sense of some of the expansion work. You know we got state approvals for the land before the accident. After that, we worked to get the experience down for the casino and resort, so we could have the architect deliver a design that supported it. We've received all the approvals for the footprint, now we're going to focus on the internal flow and design. I've included Giovanni in the planning."

"Good to hear. As soon as Chase's intel teams and security allow me to, I'll contact him. Until then, the recommendation is to stay low. I saw the email you sent with the exterior footprint and the interior outlines. It looks absolutely fantastic. You captured exactly what I envisioned, better even. The pool and swim-up bars surrounding the entire resort with gambling is fantastic. I'm really proud of what you've done, Katarina," Carlos says.

"Thanks, Dad. If you're happy with it, we'll keep moving forward," Katarina says, her blue eyes dancing with excitement, but misty with emotion. I pull her into my lap and wrap my arms around her.

"Listen, Chase told me about the meeting with the family in Italy."

She looks up at me in surprise, not realizing I've been in constant contact with him. I steady my gaze, because while she may be upset, I won't apologize for keeping her safe, and she should know that by now.

"We don't know who orchestrated the hit on us, and I don't want you anywhere near those people until we do, Katarina," Carlos says.

"I know, Dad, but it's something that I have to do. I've never had a family, and I want them to know how much the family's livelihood means to me, too, and that we can ensure they and their children to come are taken care of. You'll have to trust me. Chase has everything under control as far as security," Katarina says.

Her father sighs. "I'm sure that he does. Chase gave me an update about the meeting with your great-uncle and Giovanni. They came to visit me before they returned to Italy, but security wasn't ready to let them into the complex and turned them away. I feel bad that I couldn't see Giovanni. He's been more like a son to me over the years, having lost his father at a young age."

"I was going to ask you about him but didn't want to pry. He seemed cold at first, but before they left the meeting, he seemed to warm a bit," Katarina says.

"That would be Giovanni. He would be suspicious at first. I have no doubt once he gets to know you he'll come to love you as much as your mother and I do," her dad says, and that brings a tear to her eye.

"We'll let you know how meeting the rest of the family goes," I say, holding Katarina close, wiping a few errant tears as they spill from her eyes.

"Sounds good. I'm anxious to see if my uncle and the rest of the family accept the plan or want to continue fighting us on it. Call me once you know," Carlos says.

"Will do. Love you guys," Katarina says as I disconnect, and she turns her emotion-filled sea-colored eyes at me.

"You didn't tell me that you were in contact with my father."

"I didn't. We were discussing things that would upset you," I say.

"I don't know the half of it, do I," Katarina says, but she doesn't question, instead trusts me to take care of her, and snuggles into the protection of my arms. Something I thought may never happen, something I find priceless and that I will treasure the rest of our lives.

* * *

The plane lands, and when we settle on the tarmac, Sheldon leads us down the ramp into the sleek black limo. I assist Katarina into the back, and he jumps into the middle seat, letting the driver know we're ready once the front and rear security teams are in place for the drive to my estate.

"The security is pretty intense," Katarina says, watching the countryside out of the window as our driver navigates through the congestion, which starts to dissipate as we head toward the coastal drive that overlooks the sea.

"It is, Baby. Nothing to worry about, but necessary," I say.

She remains quiet until we reach the hilly terrain and narrow roads overlooking the vast Amalfi coastline. "Oh, my God, Chase. It's absolutely spectacular," Katarina gasps, perking up as she looks out the window, taking in the sparkling blue shimmering sea below and all the colorful homes nestled into the cliffs around and above us.

"I couldn't agree more," I say, not realizing how much I've missed the countryside and the splendor and calm that Italy brings.

I watch almost pensively for her reaction as we reach our estate, passing through the wrought iron gates and down a long winding drive that will lead us to our home in the distance. The white sprawling three-story house, with rolling green hills and acres and acres of vineyards, overlooks the sea below. "Chase, it's magnificent," Katarina says, almost breathlessly taking in the beauty around us.

I guide her out of the car, surrounded by our team of security as we walk to the front entrance.

The double-glass door is opened by Alberto, a middle-aged gentleman who has been a caretaker for the family for years and has taken care of this estate since I purchased it. "Welcome home, Chase," he says, extending his hand.

I shake it warmly. "Thank you, Alberto. This is my wife, Katarina."

"We've heard so much about you. It is a pleasure to meet you. And Gabrielle, good to see you again. Do come in," he says.

"Alberto, I hope you've been well. I'll see myself to the kitchen while everyone is getting settled. I'm looking forward to playing with a few new recipes," Gaby says, bustling past us and heading for the kitchen.

"Your baggage will be brought in. In the meantime, would you care for a glass of vino?" Alberto says, leading us through the foyer into a great room with a twenty-plus-foot ceiling decorated with ornate crown molding along its edges.

Katarina gasps at the scenery in front of us. The floor-to-ceiling windows allow a view outside to an Olympic-size infinity pool overlooking the blue-green water of the Tyrrhenian sea.

"It's absolutely incredible," Katarina says, walking to the window to get a closer look, and I am delighted that she loves it.

"Come, let's go outside on the piazza," I say, opening the French doors, taking her hand and leading her outside onto the patterned stone patio. The vast, endless rolling vineyards are nestled toward the sea as if they are growing and stretching toward it.

"I love it so much, Chase, it's hard to put into words. This is the country my father and his family came from, it is the country that your father was raised in as a boy, and a heritage that we both share," Katarina says.

The breeze feels so warm against my skin, and as I take in the majestic view in front of me and hold the woman I love close, my heart catches. "I'm so glad you like it, Baby. I've imagined what it would be like bringing you here for quite some time," I say, cuddling her from behind and lifting her hair so that I can kiss her creamy neck.

"Were you worried I wouldn't like it?" Katarina asks, nuzzling against me.

I don't answer right away, just hold her close. "I wasn't sure how you would feel about the country, given your mother's aversion to your dad's lifestyle, and in all honesty, until just this very moment, standing here with you, looking out over this vast land, I didn't know I loved it so much myself. I bought the property a few years ago because it is the most prestigious villa on the entire coast. In all honesty, maybe I'm not so different than your father. I'm not sure that I ever wanted to connect with my father's family before, but when I look out at the vineyards, the ports, the villages below, the people that depend on us, there's a connection, something I can't quite explain, but that calls to me. We'll go and visit them tomorrow," I say.

"You want to protect the people in the community like your family has always done, but maybe just in a different way," Katarina says.

I nod. "It's only just recently that I've begun to understand our families' goals. They may have been focused on turning a dollar, but the code of honor is what I find most admirable. Do you remember the salesclerk in that little store back home that we went into when we were looking for art? The woman with the black eye?"

"You mean the blonde that rang us up?"

"Yes, you may not have seen it because of the way the sun was shining into the shop, but her eye was blackened. In this country, especially here, if you hit a woman, a child, someone is going to teach you a lesson, and that's what my family would do. The community is protected by the family."

Katarina raises her eyebrows, and I don't miss the gesture.

"You may not think much of the tactics, but it is effective. Women and children should be safeguarded, not abused," I say.

She nods, just taking it in. "I certainly can't help wanting to make sure the woman is okay when she goes home," Katarina says.

"I have no doubt someone has already seen to it, Baby," I say, taking her by the hand and leading her back into the great room. The transient windows above the white French doors are open, and a massive ornate ceiling fan is moving the gentle breeze around the room. The smell of the sea is everywhere, and I inhale deeply, the aroma strangely calming to my senses. "Let me give you a tour," I say, walking my wife through the expansive stone-covered floor of the great room to the staircase beyond.

I stop at each of the rooms, but she is enthralled with the library containing floor-to-ceiling shelves filled with books on two sides of the room and the other two made of glass, overlooking the sea. I can picture her reclining on the chaise, periodically getting a glimpse of the majestic tides that crash against the coast and the sea foam that rises up while reading one of her favorite classics.

"Come, let's look, I want you to see the other rooms," I say, guiding her down a hall that is encompassed by windows all the way down the corridor, with transient windows above allowing in the natural breeze and fresh scent of the sea. I stop abruptly at the first door we reach and show her the gym.

"I know you would rather run outside, but for days that you can't," I say, gesturing toward the two newly purchased treadmills. Katarina smiles and looks up at me. I know she hates being cooped up inside, but until we get to the bottom of who attempted to kill her parents, she won't be running outside, especially when right now the suspects are her family, the very ones we've come to the country to visit.

"Thank you," Katarina says, lifting up on her toes to give me a kiss.

I place my hand on the small of her back as we walk toward the end of the hall. I open it, and her breath catches at the magnificent view of the endless turquoise sea through the open French doors and balcony that wraps around this side of the home. It's been decorated with a wrought iron table-and-chair set with a top made of stone, which sits underneath a pergola, with a fragrant purple vine and a whirlpool to the right of our room.

"Chase, it's amazing, I absolutely love it. It couldn't be more perfect," Katarina says.

I gaze down at those incredibly blue eyes, the ones that have captured my heart, and slide my hand under her hair, caressing her nape before gently pulling her toward me. "It's perfect now that you're here with me, Baby," I say, capturing her lips with my own and picking her up. Her hands instinctively wrap around my neck as I carry her into the master bedroom. The king-sized four-poster bed is old-world style, encased with gauzy material that gives it an antiquated and elegant look.

"The bed is exquisite looking, but it's so high off the ground," she says.

"Indeed, just the right height for you to need assistance getting tucked in every night, and for me to do this," I say, laying her down against the soft mattress while lifting her dress and sliding her panties past her hips and letting them glide to the floor.

Chapter 21

Gio

The meeting in Paris is infuriating. Operationally, we continue to deal with the inefficiencies caused by building space, without developing the flow of the business first. If the resort had been designed using the process Katarina outlined for the Larussio estate in Vegas, I would not be sitting in this room right now, dealing with this bullshit. "Gentlemen, I'm growing weary of having to sort situations such as this. I will be hiring a consultant to work with the team and develop suggestions for needed improvements," I say.

The manager of the resort looks indignant, as if I'm questioning his ability to handle the situation. "Emondo, rest easy, I'll pull a group in that will help uncover what we need to do to align the flow with space or determine if we need to remodel. Then we can operationalize."

He nods, and I see him visibly relax. "You are most kind," he says.

"Good, I'll let you know when I've got things arranged. In the meantime, let's take a look around," I say, and Emondo leads me out of the fiftieth-level conference room that overlooks the city of Paris, and takes me on a room-by-room tour of one of my many luxury resorts.

* * *

It is hours later before I feel confident that the team running one of my most exclusive resorts is back on track. I'll put together a summary and send it through to Torzial Consulting, the company Katarina works for, and ensure we have a plan to move forward. I board the plane, talking with the crew briefly before entering the main cabin, loosening and removing my tie, unbuttoning the top button of my dress shirt, and pouring myself a glass of wine before I settle into one of my jet's reclining seats by the window.

Antonio has kept in constant contact, giving me a play-by-play of what our security team has been able to ascertain. Serena is heading home to Italy, and her flight will arrive moments before my own does, but is scheduled to land at the public airport. I frown, wondering why the trip she's on has deviated plans from the private strip to the municipal airport, but send a text to our men to land there, too.

Two hours and twenty minutes and I will see my beauty again. I chastise myself for the thought. A grown man, one that could have any woman he wants. What the hell is so special about this woman—except everything! The way she makes my heart race, just thinking about her long dark hair, deep brown doe-like eyes, and luscious curves arouses me to no end.

The plane lifts off, and it with great restraint that I don't rub myself, conjuring up images of kissing Serena and thoughts of what it would feel like to have her squirming on the end of my cock. I take a sip of wine and enlarge the picture I have of her on my phone. So fucking beautiful, and she's not like everyone else.

She's not trying to snag onto me because she knows I'm with the Family and have money. No, instead, she's running from me and doesn't even want her brothers to see that she's associated with me.

I send a message to Antonio to make sure he is in place to take care of Serena when she lands, knowing that I'll need to get my uncle settled and on his way back to the estate before I can spend time with her alone.

We are descending when the overhead alerts go off, and the pilot comes over the speaker. "Hostile situation. We're receiving intel that we have hostiles on our tail. Prestian Corp intel is sending through messages that they've got the aggressors in sight and are advising that we land as planned. I need an executive order," the pilot says over the speaker.

"Follow whatever order Prestian Corp security gives you," I say, and my great-uncle nods his agreement.

"We've got a tail right on our ass," the pilot yells over the speaker.

"If Prestian Corp intel is on the job, they are the best in the business. Take any advice they give you," I say, walking into the security room, pulling two of the Kevlar vests that are hanging on the wall, tossing one to my great-uncle, who dons it hurriedly as I slip my arms into the other.

"Jesus, they've gotta lock," the pilot says overhead, and I look at my great-uncle and see a sense of resignation come over him as a message hits my cell from Chase Prestian's head of security.

Jay here. Head of Prestian security. Hang tight. We're handling it.

They've got a lock.

We know.

I watch as we descend, closing the space between us and the airstrip, and all of a sudden two jets fly by, one on either side of us, rocking the atmosphere mere moments before we land.

The pilot gives us an update overhead. "Enemies just flew by with someone on their tail. We're landing in two minutes. My instructions from the Prestian crew are to pull up to the public strip and not the private strip. They have eyes on the ground. Please advise."

"Do what they say," I say, looking at my great-uncle, who nods in solemn agreement.

The jet comes to a screeching halt on the strip and taxis into the public landing zone. "You okay?" I ask my great-uncle, taking his forearm to help him up.

"It's not done, Giovanni. Such an expensive air attack? Surely they'll have snipers on the ground," he says as I assist him out of the seat and into a standing position.

My cell beeps, and I read the incoming message from Jay and relay the information to my uncle. "It's being taken care of right now. They want us to stay on the plane for a few more moments," I say, knowing that we owe Chase Prestian and his team for our very existence right now.

In less then ten minutes my cell beeps again, and I read the message. My uncle is looking at me, questioning. "The snipers have been taken out, and the security team will cover us from the ramp to our car and then home. They'll have security escort you to the car. I need to stay back and handle some things," I say.

My uncle narrows his eyes at me. "Giovanni, this isn't to be taken lightly. We hit back with full force. I need you to focus on this and not on getting your dick wet," he says, his dark eyes hardened with resolve.

I clench my jaw to remain calm. My great-uncle is elder and deserves respect, but he's getting pretty fucking close to crossing the line. "Never for one minute doubt that the people who came after us won't pay. It would be a catastrophe to have all of our family in one place and give them a large target. So I've rescheduled the family meeting."

"We must protect the family at all costs," my great-uncle says.

"And we will. Chase has already set up meetings with me for tomorrow so we can figure out the next steps. The family business is being handled. In the meantime, I have some personal business to attend," I say as the plane's door opens and the Prestian Corp security team escort us to the awaiting black limo at the bottom of the ramp.

After ensuring my great-uncle is settled, I text Antonio to find out where he is and head toward the baggage claim area once he replies. A few more of the Prestian Corp security team appear and surround me as I begin walking toward the entrance of the airport. "Sir, we've been advised to secure you as quickly as possible. This is too public," one of the men says.

"We're meeting Antonio, one of my security team, and Serena. When we have them secured, we'll return to my estate," I say, following the signs through the throngs of people as they try to keep me surrounded. I see Antonio's towering six-foot-three presence, and he turns to lift a set of luggage, and Serena comes into view. She looks up and spots me, and her lovely face immediately falls, her lips purse in a tight line, and she doesn't even wait for Antonio before she heads straight for the exit.

Chapter 22

Serena

As soon as I see him striding toward me, that perfectly honed body evident under the cuts of his custom-made suit, his dark eyes glaring at me with intensity and determination, I know I need to get out of here. If he's done his research, he now knows I'm indebted to him and his family. I will pay them, that was always the plan, but the money from this flight won't get auto deposited into my bank account until next Friday. The money I've earned by taking this job will cover two months of payments and hopefully give me more time to take on additional shifts to get ahead, but he and his men are relentless, and I know that won't be good enough. My brothers have safeguarded their families to the best of their ability, and I am on my own.

I slide into the taxicab and give the driver directions, remorseful for leaving Antonio literally holding my bag. He's been so kind to me, but there is no way that I want to put him in the middle. His loyalty lies with Giovanni Larussio, as it should, and I am only the person that owes them thousands and thousands, with little hope of repaying them in the next decade.

Antonio probably has no clue, or I have no doubt the Larussios would have had him take me as collateral since the rest of my family has gone underground. I know the drill and am prepared for it. I saw the intensity in Giovanni's eyes the minute he caught sight of me.

I know it's madness, but I have to see my nonna. If I go into hiding, they will kill her, and the threats they made to me of torturing her play over and over in my head. I need to hold her hand, give her comfort, let her know that I am there for her as she struggles to recover.

The driver pulls up in front of the hospital, and I hastily wipe the tears and swipe the card payment system on the back of the seat in front of me, head into the hospital, and up the elevator to the intensive care unit.

The receptionist at the desk is friendly, and when she's cleared me for a visit, a petite olive-skinned nurse wearing blue scrubs comes to meet me and escorts me to Nonna's room. "Your grandmother is breathing on her own, although labored. She's turned a huge corner," she says, smiling at me.

"Am I able to stay awhile, sit with her?" I say.

She shines her wide smile at me. "Of course. Your brothers had to leave right before she was cleared for visitors, so she hasn't had a chance to see any of her family yet. I'm sure she will love that you are here. A couple of precautions before we go in. We need you to wash your hands and sanitize," the nurse says, gesturing to the sink.

"Of course," I say, following the instructions on the wall above the sanitizer. In a few moments, the friendly nurse leads me through double doors of glass and down a short hallway of patient exam rooms with a nursing station set in the center.

She turns and knocks lightly on one of the doors before entering. "Your granddaughter is here to visit you," she says as I skirt around her to see my nonna.

Her eyes widen, and she struggles to sit up, but I am there before she can do it on her own, helping her to adjust and lean against the headboard. "Serena, my angel. Sit by me," Nonna says, patting the bedside.

I slide in next to her, pulling her into my arms, careful to navigate the IV in her arm and the electrodes affixed to her chest. "I love you so much. I was so worried," I say, hugging her frail body against my own.

"Oh, dear girl. You worry about the oddest things. I'm an old woman and will soon be called back home. The only thing I fret about is how you will get on without me and pay the debt that should not be yours but has landed unfairly on your shoulders," she says softly.

"You don't have to worry about me at all. Those people will be paid in full very shortly," I say, cradling Nonna into my arms, swallowing back the lie, glad that her face is tucked into my body and that she will never have to think about the consequences of an Italian Mafia betrayal or the real payment they will extract.

I hold her tight for the next hour, telling her a story about the exotic island of Fiji and everything that I can remember from my research before taking a job for a customer flying to the islands. When I look down, she is fast asleep in my arms. My brothers think the worst of me, that I am some gambler who has put all of our lives in danger. I'm glad they've taken their women underground, but that leaves me, once again, all alone to take care of the family debt.

They don't realize that Nonna is in extreme danger and must be protected at all costs. I text a message to the number that I use to communicate about payment drops, letting them know that I will be late again but intend to have the money on Friday and will have it delivered at that time, before covering Nonna with a blanket and kissing her forehead.

When I get outside her door and close it behind me, I pull up Giovanni's contact, my hands shaking, hovering above it before I hit the name. She means much more to me than pride. Whatever I have is gone out the window. He answers after the second ring. "Serena."

"I know you don't owe me anything, but I'll have your family's money on Friday. I'll even be able to make a double payment. I sent a message to the person who usually collects from me, but I don't know if he will let Nonna live. I'm just asking for a few extra days, and then you'll receive double," I say.

He is quiet for so long that I don't know if he plans to answer me or just hang up. "Serena, Antonio is in the waiting room and will escort you to me. We will talk and decide how we want to proceed, but you have my word, your Nonna will be safe," Giovanni says, and with that, I willingly walk out of the safety of the ICU waiting area and into the hands of the mafia.

I glance up, and Antonio is watching me intently. "How did you get in here? It's family only," I say to the six-foot-three-inch hulk.

"I can be charming with the ladies when I need to be," Antonio says. The men have made it abundantly clear, year over year, that if they do not get their monthly payment, Nonna will suffer. I hold my head higher and straighten. As long as no harm comes to Nonna and my family, I will sell myself to the devil if that is what it takes, and if what they've threatened me with month after month is true, that may just be what it takes.

I am deep in thought as we walk down the long sterile hospital hall that will take us to the elevator, and my foot slips on the slick tile, twisting painfully underneath me. I begin to free-fall, but Antonio scoops me into his arms before I hit the floor.

He turns me and cradles me into his massive tree-trunk-like arms. I wince at the pain in my ankle, and Antonio scowls. "What hurts?" he says, looking down at me.

"I just twisted wrong, the ankle will be fine. Really, thanks for catching me, but I can walk on my own," I say as we reach the elevator.

"Sorry, Serena. I'm partial to my balls, which means me Caveman and you Jane until we can have someone take a look at that ankle," Antonio says, hitting the button for the lower level that will connect us with the outdoor world, cabs, and hotel rooms.

Antonio shifts me in his arms, and as the door opens, all I see is the overwhelming and scowling glare of the man that everyone in Italy knows will take over the vast empire of the Larussios when his great-uncle passes.

I take a deep breath as Antonio walks us out of the elevator. "She hurt her ankle. She shouldn't walk on it until we get it looked at," he says, seemingly unaffected by that glare.

Giovanni's features soften as he looks down at me, his eyes full of concern. This dark-eyed Adonis reaches for me. His hand snakes out, sliding behind my neck, his fingers caressing my nape as he lifts me into his arms.

I inhale his scent deeply as he tucks me closer to him. I should be scared, not knowing what he intends to do with me, but he has been nothing but kind to me, and he has promised that no harm will come to my nonna. I feel nothing but protected as he walks us to the awaiting Lincoln outside the hospital doors and slides into the seat with me still in his arms.

Chapter 23

Katarina

Chase has introduced me to the beauty of his homeland, with a brief bit of time spent drinking coffee overlooking the vineyards, taking long walks along our private seafront and the lemon groves, and just enjoying the serenity and getting to know his family.

We have been swimming in the sea for over an hour when Chase guides me out of the water and up the private stone path toward the outdoor shower.

He turns the spray on and pulls me under the mist as we rinse off the sand from our bodies.

"Turn a little. If this sand goes into the house, you may not end up with one of Gaby's desserts tonight," I say, taking the hose from him and dousing his skin with it.

He smirks, looking down at me with those deep green eyes. "Indeed, it would be a shame if I were forced to get my sweet fix another way. Perhaps I would have to undress you, tie you to our bed, and lap the sugar from between your legs until I get to that creamy center."

Just the thought causes my center to moisten with desire for this man. I smile up at him as he undresses me with his heated gaze.

"Your nipples are hard, and if our security team weren't watching, I'd slide my finger in and find you soaked, wouldn't I?" Chase asks.

I nod. "So wet right now. I'm pretty sure you're going to have to have double dessert tonight," I say.

He grins at me, and then scowls as his phone beeps, answering it as I pat dry and pull on my cover-up for the walk up to the house.

Chase signals for the guards and places his hand around me, guiding me quickly up the path, forgetting all about his shower until we are in the entryway. "Go into the house, Katarina, get dressed quickly," he says, closing the door behind me as I enter the foyer.

I slip out of my cover-up and suit, slip into my robe, throw my clothes into the laundry basket, and head inside.

"Hurry, Katarina, we need to head into the safe room. Step onto this towel and make sure your feet are completely dry," Gaby says. I dry my feet on the towel and she leads me down the hall to the dining room. "Chase and the boys will handle whatever's happening, but they want us far away from the chaos."

Whatever is happening, there is no point in arguing. Chase will do what he feels necessary to protect those around him, regardless of my protests, which are almost nonexistent, having realized that his highly skilled security team know things before they happen.

I follow Gaby through the dining room, and as we enter the great room, she pulls a book off of a shelf and pushes a button behind it, replacing it before the case begins to turn, opening into an entryway that we walk into just as the overhead alarm alerting us that we have visitors goes off overhead.

"What is that?" I ask as the bookcase closes behind us and she guides me into the elevator.

"Go in, it will take us underground. The house is set on a hill for a reason," Gaby says as we descend.

As the doors open, and we walk through. I'm not even surprised that the space in front of us is the exact replica of the area on the floor above us. Eerily identical, the same bookcase-turned-door, the dining room replicated to a tee. Holy fuck, the design of the house may be completely different than our house in Chicago overlooking Lake Michigan, but it feels strangely the same. All the comforts of home for as long as Chase and his security team deem it necessary for us to remain downstairs. If I snoop around, I'm sure to find a room with a group of men monitoring screens and communication waves to ensure our safety is guaranteed.

"Come, child, better not to worry about what you can't change. Chase and Sheldon will be down when they can. In the meantime, go and change in your bedroom and then let's make the boys some pizzas," Gaby says with a spark in her eyes.

I nod, knowing Chase will be down as soon as possible and that she lives for putting smiles on the security guards' faces with her fabulous meals. "You got it," I say, heading down that hallway that would lead me to our bedroom upstairs, and sure enough, it does. When I turn the handle on our double-doored suite, a king-sized four-poster bed similar to the one upstairs greets me. There is a large picture of the sea and an electric fireplace in the corner for coziness.

I open the walk-in closet door and find clothing, all my favorites. I open the vertical drawers and pull out panties, a sports bra, and leggings, slipping them on before pulling on a t-shirt. I check my phone to see if I have a message from Chase. Nothing.

I trust him implicitly and no longer have the desire or need to know exactly what's happening every minute, but I do need our connection, and to know he's alright. That I can't negotiate, so I send him a message, knowing that our phones are entirely untraceable but fully aware we still need to be careful with communications.

I'm safe, are you okay?

Yes, nothing to worry about, Baby. I'll see you soon.

I tuck my phone into my pocket and head toward the kitchen, which is top-of-the-line, with stainless steel Sub-Zero appliances all around the perimeter. I take note of the commercial-grade stove built into the stone walls and a refrigerator that looks so large it should belong in a restaurant, and the custom-made wine cooler underneath the granite counter.

"Apron is on the back of the door," Gaby says, reminding me of my promise to assist cooking for Chase and the security team.

I don the white smock with a picture of a chef's hat on it and try to get in the mood to cook. "Okay, tell me what you need me to help with," I say, twisting my hair into a messy bun.

"Same drill as before. The dough is rising. Why don't you cut the peppers and onions, and wash and dry the mushrooms while I get the sausage sautéed?" Gaby says.

"Sure, you make it sound easy. Cut this, do that. And which peppers am I supposed to cut?" I ask teasingly as I slip on a pair of gloves and eye the overflowing basket of colored peppers.

"Green, red, and yellow will do. Colorful and flavorful. Just dice them like we did for the last pizzas we made," Gaby says.

I smile as she bustles around the kitchen. Gaby has been with Chase for seven years, taking care of him after his own mother died and ensuring that his homes and meals are taken care of. She has become like a second mother to him, and as dear as any mother-in-law could be to me.

"Sure, let's do this," I say, taking one of the knives out of the block and slowly but efficiently begin to chop the vegetables for the pizza that is planned for later on this evening.

I am spreading Gaby's sauce on the crusts when I sense him. The magnetism of his gaze never ceases to pull me in its direction, ensuring that he has my undivided attention.

I slide my gloves off, leaving them in the sink, and rush into his arms. "It's okay, Baby. We had company, but nothing we weren't expecting. No need for concern," Chase says.

I narrow my eyes at him. "Which means you don't want to tell me about it," I say.

His deep green eyes do not leave me as they watch me work this through. "I think you already know the answer to your question, Katarina. I will always want to protect you. Anything else you need to ask?" Chase says.

All the initial misunderstandings because I couldn't entirely place my trust in Chase are gone. There's nothing of the old questions, and it is a great relief, but I am still a woman, and being kept in the dark still sometimes rankles. "No, I trust you with our lives," I say, reaching up on my tiptoes, grasping my hands around his nape, pulling him down closer, feeling the warmth of his breath before I take his lips with my own.

I hear his groan one second before I am being lifted in the air and carried out of the safe room and into our bedroom upstairs. He shuts the door with his foot and turns, sliding me up the wall, his hands grasping my hips to hold me steady as I wrap my legs around him. I hear the unbuckling of a belt and his pants drop to the floor one second before his finger pushes the satiny material of my panties aside.

"So wet, so responsive, Baby. Tell me you trust me to keep you safe," Chase says, whispering in my ear as he rubs the wetness he has created up and down my center with his cock before penetrating me so deep that it causes me to cry out with pleasure. His need is intense and all-consuming and he continues kissing and sucking the length of my neck with fierce abandon, creating goosebumps all over my body. He moves fast and furiously, in time with our growing need, thrusting deep, hitting the exact spot, the one that causes me to moan again and again, and when he tells me to come, wave after wave overtake me as he powers through them, prolonging my pleasure as he releases deep inside of me.

I am still breathless as his lips capture mine with intensity, and he carries me to our bed. "Mine, and I protect what's mine," Chase says, pulling me into his arms and caressing the tops of my shoulders as our breathing starts to return to normal.

I don't ask him any questions, although it's clear something has him worked up. I snuggle into his arms and am surprised when he starts talking.

"Your great-uncle and I have been in constant contact. The meetings have been pushed out to ensure our families are safe, but after today, we are in a better position. The family will gather tomorrow night," Chase says.

"Oh, my God. That's too soon! I need time to prepare," I say, sitting straight up in bed. He pulls me down and folds me back into his arms.

"You are a Larussio by blood, you are a Prestian by marriage, and you instinctively have exactly what it takes to go head-to-head with the person that is threatening our lifestyle and your father's vision. I have complete faith in you, but our security will need to triple after today," Chase says, and I know now if I didn't already that whatever happened is still a dangerous threat.

Chapter 24

Chase

In the morning, Katarina is engrossed in preparing for the meeting with her family in what used to be my office but has now been taken over with the Larussio Vegas plans. I call Jay to get another report on the attack.

"It's some of the Chicago men, Chase, but the thing about it is they aren't getting their direction from Bernatelli. I've got our intel working on it, and Scottie's got a few leads out through Interpol. The good thing is that we drew them out, we know who they are and have communication locks on them. They make a move or say a word over the waves, and we're monitoring it all. Right now, they're trying to stay low, so we don't find them. Dumbfucks don't even know that we're watching them. It's the safest window of time to get together if we're going to do this," Jay says.

"We are, but triple Katarina's security. No one gets near her, Jay," I say. My first instinct was to keep her away from the meeting, have her use Skype or whatever fucking technology we have to keep her protected, but I know she won't accept that. She is strong and willful and would find a way into the meeting, probably ending with her trying to give the security team the slip, and that we can't have right now. I smile at the need to be one step ahead of my spirited wife, but it is short-lived. I know that to protect her, we need to tell her what we know. I've kept it from her for too long, waiting for proof. I look down at my cell and grimace.

Where are you?

No time like the present.

Downstairs, in the communications room. Take the elevator. Will meet you.

She reaches the lower level, and I am waiting for her, avoiding the question in her eyes, instead guiding her toward the door at the end of the hall. I slide the magnetic card over the keypad, and it engages a computer display. In under thirty seconds, it has recognized my retinal image, and we have gained entry into the communications room.

She's seen these men before, the same ones that came to the Prestian estate in Chicago when we learned her mother had been kidnapped by Alfreita. The team that runs the private communications intel operation for Prestian Corp and are broadening their scope to include Carrington Steel and Katarina's entire Italian side of the family.

As the door closes, a few men look up and nod, but they don't remove their headsets, and some are too engrossed in the multiple monitors in front of them to even look up. There is a small group around a large monitor tucked away in the corner, and Jay's voice comes over the speaker system. I pull out a chair and gesture for Katarina to take a seat.

"Glad you were able to join us, Kate," Jay says, using her shortened name. "Men, as you know, we had visitors yesterday. Appreciate your diligence in alerting us to the fact that they may have been coming before they got anywhere near the villa, and your work in getting locks on their whereabouts last night and today.

We've got a ton of heat coming our way, and it's not as simple as we first thought. I think we'll have positive identities very soon.

"Thanks, Jay, stay on it, and let me know what the team learns as they investigate. Are we prepared for this evening?" I ask, squeezing Katarina's hand.

"We are. Taps have been placed in the Larussio dining room, kitchen, great room, patio, and the conference room you and Kate will be meeting the family in. The communications room was impenetrable, so we'll have to get that intel via satellite."

"Excellent. Great work. Jay, let me know when you find out. In the meantime, I'll leave you and your team to the details," I say, taking Katarina's hand and guiding her out of the communications center and onto the elevator that will take us back upstairs.

She was quiet downstairs, but not so much anymore. "What the hell is going on, Chase? I thought the people that had a fix on the house last night were the Larussio family. They weren't?" she asks me as we reach the dining room.

"No, Baby, in fact, some of your family were caught on surveillance ensuring the people trying to get onto our property never even got close to the gates of our villa."

"Holy hell!" Katarina says, pacing back and forth.

"We'll know more soon. In the interim, we need to follow through with our original plan. You need to meet with your great-uncle and the entire family, give them an update on Carlos's condition and the status of the Vegas builds and the revenue it's anticipated to produce. If you do this, our intel teams will be able to follow the facial expressions of everyone in the room, anyone they contact after that, and—" I start to say, but she cuts me off.

"I've got it. We need to draw out whoever is watching us," Katarina says, and I wish to hell that I could keep her safely in the estate and not right in the middle of what will most definitely be an intense and eye-opening evening for everyone involved.

Chapter 25

Gio

When the elevator door opens and Antonio walks out holding Serena in his arms, he almost signed his death warrant. He's damn lucky he was just protecting what's mine, but she's not staying in another man's arms any longer than necessary, and I quickly take her from him, pulling her body tightly against my own as we walk her to the car.

Her arms tighten around my neck, and she nuzzles into my chest, and when we reach the Lincoln, while I could easily place her onto the seat beside me without hurting her ankle, I don't. Instead, I pull the seat belt around the two of us, keeping her pressed tightly to my chest, focused on her breathing as Antonio gets in beside the driver and gives him directions to the most exclusive hotel on the Amalfi Coast, one of my favorite properties and where I sometimes stay while in the city.

"Jay's security team wanted an update on where we were going so they could clear the area. I have one of our men walking them through the penthouse right now," Antonio says.

I nod, appreciative of the extra precautions that Chase Prestian is providing, but right now I can only concentrate on the beauty in my lap. There are so many things I want to talk to her about, but before I do, I need answers, and while my team is working furiously to get them, it is not fast enough.

I look down, and she's watching me with those deep brown eyes, but dark shadows surround her saddened eyes. I'm sure the last time she slept decently was on the plane from New York to Italy, before she knew of her nonna's condition. Instead, she has been on another back-to-back overseas flight, tending to other people's needs instead of being with her nonna, where she belonged.

I push a straggling piece of her long dark hair from her eyes and gently close her lids. "Sleep, Tesoro," I say, and she nuzzles into my chest without fear or question, and my chest tightens with something that I've never felt before and can't quite comprehend.

I hear and feel the beep on my phone and dig it out of my pocket while trying not to disturb her. I glance at the message, and my jaw tightens. Not one of the family heads has Serena or her nonna on the list of people that owe us money. Someone has to have her on the list, and that very same person has threatened an old lady if payment is not made. We don't do business like that, and every single one of us knows that, but whoever has, their time in this world is drawing to a very rapid end.

When the driver pulls up to my hotel, Antonio gets out and holds the door for me as I unbuckle us and walk with Serena in my arms through the grand lobby and toward the private elevator that will open on the penthouse floor. She is exhausted and doesn't even stir as we ride up the elevator. "The floor has been cleared, and your physician is on the way. I'm going to go down and meet him, or Prestian's security team won't let him up," Antonio says.

"Thanks for finding her and taking care of her at the hospital," I say.

"You're welcome, Giovanni," Antonio says, pushing the button that will take him downstairs, leaving me alone with my dark-haired beauty. I carry her without thought to my bed. One that no woman has ever seen and that she is not yet cleared to be in, but I'll be damned if she's going back to her home alone after what she told me.

I settle her onto my bed, and as soon as I remove her from my arms, her beautiful lips turn downward in the cutest pout and her eyes blink trying to open. "It's okay, Serena. Go back to sleep, Tesoro," I say, taking her hand in my own. She calms and turns her cheek into my hand, and my chest tightens again with the knowledge that she felt safe and protected with me, even though someone has threatened her in the vilest of ways, the life of her nonna, the one person she cares everything about.

I glance up as Antonio and Luco walk in. I lay Serena's hand down, and her lip moves down again, and it's all I can do not to grin like a fool in front of my security guard and physician. "Thanks for coming on such short notice, Luco. Can you check her ankle?" I say.

"Of course, Antonio told me what happened. Slickly polished floors and stick heels, not a good combination," he says, walking toward her and gently grasping the still heeled left foot. She grimaces and opens her eyes wide as he starts to unbuckle her sandal. I take her hand in mine. "Lucas is my personal physician. He'll be careful with your ankle, Serena," I say.

She nods, but as he moves her ankle around and slides his finger along the bones, her lips tighten into a thin line. "While I don't think it's broken, she's swelling and already bruising. My team should be arriving with the mobile x-ray unit in a few moments, they were held up by your security men," Luco says to me.

"Security is tight for the entire family right now," I say, and he nods.

Antonio glances down at his phone. "They're on the way up," he says right before the ding of the elevator alerts us to their arrival. Two men are escorted into the room by Antonio and another security guard who doesn't look happy with the situation at all. "Everyone that stays in the room wears a radiation vest," Luco says, placing one over the top of Serena.

I slide one on because I'm not leaving her alone. Her naturally red lips part in a smile all for me. "You can leave," I say to the guards, and they do, except for Antonio, who throws a vest on. "Alright, you ready for this Serena?" he says, looking down at her.

She nods and gives him a shy smile while they put her foot on a pillow and position it. She grimaces and squeezes my hand hard when they turn it. "Easy, Serena, it'll be over in a moment," I say, rubbing her palm with my finger.

They take the pictures they need and send them electronically to the radiologist, who will read them. Luco talks with her, asking her a few questions, and in less then ten minutes has the results. "Good news. It's not broken, but it is severely sprained. See all the bruising already occurring?" he says. "We need to get the swelling down. I'm going to lightly splint you just to keep you immobile, and then you're going to need to stay off your foot and keep it elevated until the swelling resolves. No walking, or it will take longer to heal," he says.

"I can't be immobile. I have to go back to work. There is no option."

"Serena, you will stay here for the next couple weeks, and we'll talk once we're alone," I say to her.

Her eyes glisten with unfallen tears, and she struggles to hold them back. My jaw clenches tightly with the realization that the weight of the world has fallen on her shoulders. She does not succumb to tears but instead nods her agreement.

"Very good," Luco says. "Keep the ankle elevated and iced. I'll leave something with Giovanni for your pain."

"Thank you so much," Serena says.

"You're very welcome. I'll stop by in a few days. Until then, rest, ice and elevate," Lucas says, taking his bag and heading out the door with his x-ray technicians and the security team.

"You didn't have to take care of me," Serena says, sliding up on the pillow and leaning against the headboard. She is still in her uniform top and skirt, and I realize she hasn't even had a chance to change and probably hasn't had a chance to shower since she left the hospital for her flight. She went from taking care of people on the plane, and then straight to her nonna.

"Serena, let me take care of you and then we'll talk about the payments you owe."

Her eyes lower in embarrassment, but she nods her agreement. I send a note to my shopper to bring her clothes and a message to Antonio to have the packages brought up as soon as they arrive.

"Right now, I want you to take one of these capsules," I say, handing her a glass of water. "Then we're going to get you into a bubble bath where you can relax for a little bit until your clothes arrive," I say.

She looks up at me with widened brown eyes, and my first thought is that the fear of me has returned, but instead her eyes look hazy and full of wonder. She's just confused and taking it all in. "Stay here," I say, and leave her to go and run a warm bath, filling it with the fragrant scented oil that's always on the ledge but I've never bothered with before.

When I return, she's managed to get out of her uniform jacket, and the thinness of her blouse provides me with a look at the beautiful curves of her breasts. My need to take care of her hasn't been well thought-out. "Come, I'll carry you into the bathroom and set you on the ledge. You can get undressed and then cover yourself with a towel while I put you in the tub," I say.

Her breath audibly catches, and her eyes have turned hazy, the same look like right before I kissed her. She nods, and that's all the consent I need, scooping her into my arms and carrying her to the bathroom. I lower her gently onto the ledge, turning her so I can place her ankle on a small chair I've brought into the bathroom. "There, I'll give you a few moments, and if you need anything, I'll be right outside the door," I say, placing her phone onto the ledge beside her.

"Thank you," she says softly as I turn and head out the door. My cock is straining hard against the zipper. She's so fucking responsive and submissive, and she is completely mine, whether she knows it or not. I wait impatiently outside the door, imagining her undressing until my cell beeps with a message from Jay.

We have the bastards. We know who they are and need to draw them out. Family meeting?

Great work. Yes, set it up on your end. I'll have the family gathered.

Roger that.

"I'm ready, Gio," Serena says from beyond the bathroom door, and I lose all interest in meetings as I open the door. She's sitting on the edge of my bathtub with just a small towel held across her curvaceous breasts and is holding a washcloth across her mound. My breath hitches and my cock throbs hard. I try to focus on her eyes instead of that lush body, but the curves of her hips visible around her hand holding that little washcloth couldn't be more enticing if she were trying.

"Hang onto my neck. I'll lift you and set you into the water," I say, picking Serena up and lowering her into the water so she can keep her foot elevated. "When you get done, let me know, and I'll help you out. I've asked the shopper to bring you a robe and nightgowns that won't require much effort to get into with your ankle. I would bring you a glass of wine, but not with the medicine, Tesoro. Enjoy the bubbles and let me know when you're ready to get out," I say, spinning and closing the door.

I am replaying the image of my dark-haired beauty in my head, rubbing my cock through my pants, when she lets out a scream that sends a chill right through my heart.

I hear Serena scream again and I burst through the bathroom door. "Do whatever you want to me, but let her go. She's done nothing. She's old, and she can't get you the money, but I can. I just need more time! I told you that. Please, please let her go," Serena yells at me, sobbing. I hear the elevator open and know my security team has been privy to the commotion. I open the door and tell them to stay out before I close the door in their face. No one sees her like this.

"Serena, calm down. I don't know what you're talking about. Is it your nonna?" I ask, walking toward her, but she shrivels herself up against the stone tile, as far from me as humanly possible, and I cringe at the look of pure fear in her eyes. She suddenly realizes she's naked and grabs the small towel and places it across the swell of her breast not covered by the bubbles.

"I don't have anything to do with anyone threatening her, and I'm trying to find out who is. Believe me, Serena, and tell me what just happened," I say.

She cowers, and I think she's not going to respond, but then she hands me her phone with trembling hands. I turn it over and read the message that is still prominently displayed.

Every late day the old woman loses a digit.

The rage I feel is indescribable. If someone in our family is threatening her, they are dead, and if someone outside of our family is threatening her, they will live to regret it, suffering a prolonged and painful death. "Stay here, I need to get someone on this right now," I say, and she draws in a large breath, and her dark eyes turn hopeful.

"I love her so much," she says, and tears continue to fall, marring her beautiful face. It is with difficulty that I leave her in this state, but if we don't move fast, someone could take her nonna, if they haven't already.

I close the door behind me and catch Antonio. "Someone's threatening Serena's grandmother. Trace this number, do it quickly."

"We'll take care of it. I left two men at the hospital, and they haven't reported anything wrong, so they're probably just trying to scare her," Antonio says, dropping the bags of clothing I've had purchased onto the dining room table.

"Get ahold of them and find out for sure," I say, and Antonio hits the button on his phone that will connect him to the rest of the team.

"We can split up and head over to check on her, too," Cole, one of the Prestian Corp security members says.

"Yes, I would appreciate that. Keep in touch with Antonio."

Antonio gets off the phone and shakes his head. "They just checked on her, she's sleeping like a baby. The fuckers are just trying to intimidate her."

"They'll be expecting her to find the money somehow. Set up a payment drop with these assholes, find out who they are, and bring them to me before the night is through," I say, handing Antonio her phone as I walk back into the bathroom, and they head down the elevator.

She has her head on her one raised knee when I walk in and turns to look at me. "Tesoro, your nonna is sleeping right now and heavily guarded. No one will get near her, and my men are going to find the person that threatened her. Tomorrow, I want you to tell me the entire story, but for now, we're going to dry you off, get you into a clean nightgown, and you are going to sleep," I say, and while I thought she would protest, she merely nods.

I hold a small dry towel to her hands to allow her to cover herself as I lift her out, but it falls into the bathtub, and she makes no attempt to retrieve it, her eyes becoming heavy and glazed with tiredness. Instead, she snakes her hands around my neck as I lift her, being careful to keep her ankle immobile. I press her beautiful body to me and place her on the chair I've brought in. Stay here, dry off while I get your robe." When I return, Serena has her hair wrapped in a towel and has patted dry, and is modestly covering her breasts and mound from my eyes. The little bit of material doesn't hide her curvaceous hips and long thighs, though, or the length of her neck and curves of her shoulders. The tender flesh that I am dying to feel against my own.

My dick throbs hard with the need for this woman, but it will have to wait. Instead, I hold out the robe for her to slip her arms into, allowing her privacy to cover herself and tie the garment. "There, now, let's dry your hair and then off to bed you go," I say, pulling a blow-dryer from the cabinet, unwrapping her long dark tresses, and beginning to comb through her hair, drying each strand until it is once again smooth and silky. I search in the cupboard for a spare toothbrush and put some paste on it and hand it to her before scooting her chair to the sink.

She blushes and my dick throbs. "Brush, Tesoro, and then I'll put you to bed," I say. When she's done, I lift her, carrying her to my bed, placing her foot on top of the pillow. I go for ice while she settles, and when I return she is sound asleep. I push the hair from her eyes and cover her with the blankets and arrange her injured ankle on a towel covering the ice.

I could watch her sleeping in my bed all night, but pull myself away and head into the shower, trying not to think about her luscious curves, that were just in this very same bathroom. Instead, I get in and out, throw a towel around my waist, and hit Antonio's number while I walk into the dining room and pour myself a drink. "Any word?" I say.

"They just accepted a drop. The fuckers think Serena's still in Naples and want to meet her in the alley behind old town. Nothing good happens in that part of town. We've got men in the area that will handle it."

"Bastards. Let me know when it's done and that you have them secured. Let them hang in fear overnight," I say, disconnecting.

In less than an hour, Antonio calls me with an update. The men have been apprehended. A small-time gang from up the coast, who apparently have been using our name to put the fear of god into helpless women and families.

I don't even have time to deal with anything because Jay is sending me message after message about the attempt on my life and that of my great-uncle. They've been able to get a lock on the men but they haven't come out, and they haven't got confirmation on who they are just yet.

The light of the moon is shining into the floor-to-ceiling windows, and I watch as Serena sleeps, her soft inhalations of breath and movement of her chest keeping me mesmerized. She is perfection, and with that, I curl up against my pillow and watch her until sleep finally overtakes me.

I wake to the sound of crying, long drawn out sobs of despair. "No, we paid, you promised," Serena yells, tossing and turning, struggling against the binds of her sheets and blankets.

I am wide awake in a minute and slide my hand beneath her

nape, grasping her hand with the other. "Serena, wake up, you're dreaming, Tesoro. Nonna is okay," I say, pulling her against me. She finally stops struggling and listens. "Your nonna is fine. She's sleeping, and the men that threatened her have been picked up. It's over," I say, and she lets out a long sob and begins crying hard, burying her face into my chest.

"Tell me, Serena," I say, wiping her tears as quickly as they fall.

"It's been years, and just like that, it's over," Serena says, and my blood pumps hard with fury.

"You need to tell me what you mean by that," I say.

She chokes back her sobs, and I'll give her time, but she'll tell me what I want to know before I let her leave my bed. She's crying softly and her tears are wet against my chest and with every tear spilled I vow that whoever has created this amount of fear in my dark-haired beauty will pay dearly for that act.

I stroke her nape, caressing her and rub the inside of her palm with my finger. She eventually starts to calm and uses her free hand to wipe her tears. "It was a long time ago. My grandfather borrowed money to rebuild the family business after a fire took it to the ground. He didn't have the collateral to go to the bank, so he went to the Larussios. Nonna said he thought they were always fair in their business dealings and had protected many of the people in the community. They gave him a fair price for the loan, and he started monthly payments. He was making the payments on time until something happened and they killed him," Serena says, inhaling deeply and wiping the tears that have spilled down her cheeks.

"They came to the house one night and gave Nonna a check to pay off our home. They told her the debt would be taken care of. She went to the bank the next day and paid off the house with the money they'd given her. The very next night she received a phone call telling her that they were setting up a payment plan to recover not only the money they had given her to pay the house. Also, thousands of dollars that my grandfather accrued in gambling debt while he was trying to find the money to rebuild the business."

"I'm looking into this, Serena. I don't know what happened just yet, but understand this. You and your nonna owe nothing to our family. Whatever happened, consider the debt cleared and the people that are threatening your nonna, they are not my family. I don't know who they are just yet, but I will by tomorrow. You are free from this worry, do you understand? Never will you ever fret about your nonna's safety after today," I say, and she wraps her hands around my waist and nuzzles into my chest.

"I don't know how to thank you. I grew up fearing you," Serena says, looking up at me with those wide velvety brown eyes.

I push her hair aside so I can bare her neck and gently stroke it. She moans softly and my cock hardens.

"I like the way you touch me," she says softly, slipping the delicate strands of her camisole over her shoulders, baring her breasts to me in the moonlit room before leaving soft kisses on my bare chest.

I was trying to hold back, but this woman is a passionate Italian woman, and I do intend to satisfy her every need and taste my beauty.

I capture her hands and push them over her head and toward the headboard. "Keep them here or I will punish you. Do you understand, Tesoro?" I ask, watching her eyes, the color and emotion just barely visible through the dim light of the room. I can't help myself, her lips, those luscious red lips part, and I capture them, kissing her, tasting her sweetness as she opens for me and my tongue finds hers.

"I want you, Giovanni," she says as I make my way from her

lips, across her creamy neck, and lower to find the hardened tips of her breasts.

She moans softly as I lick and suck, and then cries out with pleasure when I increase the pressure. My dick thickens with desire, knowing how completely compatible we are, and while I would like nothing better than to feel her warmth, I want our first time joined to be special, but her body is aroused and I kiss down it, teasing her navel, feeling her tight belly tense as I make my way lower. Her panting is intoxicating, and I adjust myself so I can lie between her legs, parting her thighs, licking up them as I do.

"Tell me what you want," I say and she doesn't say a word, instead she lifts her hips, presenting her pussy to me.

"Tell me what you want," I repeat.

"I want to feel you there, your kisses, everything, Gio," Serena says and with that I let my tongue wash over her clit and taste my dark-haired beauty for the very first time.

She clenches the bedsheets, pushing her hips up to meet me as I explore her satiny folds, dipping into her center, licking her little clit over and over, causing her to cry out with need. I will allow her anything tonight, but tomorrow she will learn the rules, and my cock hardens at the thought of teaching her as her body begins to tremble on the end of my tongue as I continue to lick her through her pleasure.

I shift myself on the bed so I can hold her in my arms as her pulse slowly begins to normalize, stroking her hair and her neck. My cock is hard, thick and raging, but her body is coming down from her high, and she sighs deeply, turning and nuzzling her face into my chest, and I hold her close as she drifts off to sleep.

* * *

It is hours later when I feel the bed shift and open my eyes, but not before my dark-haired beauty has decided to take matters into her own hands. She grabs hold of the footboard and then begins to hop on her left foot, trying to make her way to the bathroom. I'm up in a flash, and she's reached about a third of the way before her leg gives out, and I scoop her into my arms.

"I told you I would take care of you. All you had to do was wake me and tell me your needs. Now you'll have a reddened ass for your trouble," I say, carrying her to the bathroom. Daylight is starting to stream into the room, and it's not my imagination that her eyes widen with that same desire I saw on the plane. I push the bathroom door open and set her carefully on the toilet. "I'll give you some privacy, although you don't deserve it, and go and get your medicine ready. I"ll be back shortly," I say.

I hear the toilet flush, and when I return, her olive colored cheeks are rosy with embarrassment, and my dick strains against my lounge pants. She glances down, and her eyes dilate. I scoop her up and hold her in my arms so she can wash her hands before taking her back to bed and settling her in. "Eat first, it will coat your stomach," I say, holding the delicate pastry to her mouth. She tentatively bites a piece and chews and then takes another. She is hungry, and in a short amount of time has consumed the entire half. I hold her medicine out and a glass of orange juice and she puts her hands around it, swallowing both her medicine and juice. "There, let's get you tucked back into bed," I say, settling her, and propping her ankle back onto the pillow and heading into the kitchen to get some fresh ice.

I walk back into the room, and her dark eyes are watching me. "Do you think I could call Nonna? She's always up at this time having a coffee," Serena says.

I google the hospital number and connect before handing the phone to Serena. "Here you go, Tesoro. While you talk, you need to keep your foot iced and say nothing about the family. The hospital phones aren't secure," I say.

She nods and surprises me by placing the phone on speaker before leaning her head back into the pillows as she speaks to the receptionist who rings her through. "Hello," a frail voice finally says and Serena's entire body relaxes.

"Nonna, I miss you so much. How are you doing?" she says as I head to the kitchen to see what we have stocked and what I'll want to be ordered in for the next couple of weeks. When I'm finished and almost at the bedroom door, I hear her talking gently and I can't help but stop and listen from outside the door.

"Okay, I'll tell you all about this trip. We could see the sprawling greenish-blue ocean from the air and the entire time the plane was taxiing. We were mesmerized by the island's different colors and sandy white beaches. When we landed, we were ushered to cabins with glass walls linked together by bridges. It was the most exotic thing you've ever seen, and the greenery, lushness like you could never imagine."

"I love it when you tell me about all of your trips. I'm so happy that you have such a wonderful life. Do you know where your brothers are? They haven't been to see me, and I've tried to ring them with no answer," Nonna says as I walk back in the room, and Serena's eyes drop, and her lips tighten.

"They were with you when you were taken to the hospital because I was still on the flight back to Italy from America, but they had to go back to work once I arrived. I'll give them a call and see if they can arrange a trip south to see you, Nonna," Serena says.

"That would be lovely," her nonna says before they say their goodbyes and Serena disconnects. Her eyes are starting to haze with tiredness from the meds, but they are drenched in sadness.

I sit beside her, and my hand moves to her nape, caressing her, needing to feel our connection and she nuzzles into my hand. "She thinks they don't care enough to visit, and it's all my fault. I never told them anything. I didn't want them to risk their lives and their families', so I never told them or asked for help," Serena says.

"You were protecting your family, Serena, there is nothing dishonorable about that," I say, raising her chin so she will look at me. "Tell me, where are your brothers and their families," I say, and tears begin to pool in her gorgeous brown eyes.

"They didn't tell me, they couldn't trust me, they thought I was the one that owed the debt that brought trouble to their families," she says, and I make a mental note to send a message to Antonio and Jay to find her brothers. They are her brothers, they should have known something was amiss. They should have done so many things for her, and she may be forgiving of their ignorance and desertion, but I am not.

"Relax, or read, and don't worry. Going forward, you have no problems, understand, Tesoro?" It is with difficulty that I don't slip in beside to hold her, but there is much to do. The first order of business is to have my team find out who the people are that threatened her grandmother and have been extorting money from them for years, and the second is to find out who the hell has a target on the backs of the Larussios.

I walk into the kitchen and pour myself a cup of coffee, fire up the laptop, and dig into the never-ending emails, plowing through them when the message I've waited for arrives. I read it and then reread it. Antonio's team has done well, but the thought that there are many more families out in the country that believe we are extorting money from them makes me seethe with anger. "They stay alive until we have the entire list, every single family they're extorting money from," I text.

It is hours later, and still no definitive word from Jay about the source of the snipers when I go to check on Serena for the third time. The medication has made her dozy and she reads for a bit and then falls asleep. She is awake when I walk in with lunch and settles herself against the headboard of the bed as I arrange the meal tray across her lap.

"Thank you for taking care of me," she says before taking a bite of the creamy mushroom risotto.

"You're welcome," I say, settling into the chair in the corner with a bowl of my own.

"It's very good," she says, taking another taste.

"I couldn't agree more," I say, watching her eat and glance my way every once in awhile. The attraction I feel for this woman is intense, and I push down the urge to slide into bed with her and make her my very own. I know she feels it too, her cheeks flush when I look at her, and I can see the pulse of her neck from here. She has to get better, and I need to find out who the hell is responsible for this if we are to ever get past this.

She places her fork on the tray and wipes her mouth daintily with the napkin. "It was so filling. I'm getting a little tired again," Serena says.

"Close your beautiful eyes and go to sleep," I say as I take her tray, and her head lolls against the pillow. In less than five minutes, she is fast asleep with her hair splayed out in my bed. I have no idea what to think of her, but one thing I know is that she belongs to me now and I will not let her go.

It is with regret, later, that I have to leave Serena in the hands of the Prestian Corp security and Antonio. There is no way I can get out of the family meeting without causing all-out war, and after reading Uncle Carlos's living will and hearing the presentation that Katarina gave, I know that I need to be there to support my cousin in her attempt to bring her father's wish to fruition.

I walk into the conference room, glancing around the massive table already filled with my cousins, uncles, and great-uncle, and take a seat. In less than twenty minutes of listening to Katarina talk, I find myself blowing up at the stupidity surrounding me and find myself looking straight down the barrels of two high-end Glocks.

Chapter 26

Katarina

I will face the entire Larussio family today, attempting to convince them that my father is not the enemy, that he has their best interests at heart, that he would do anything, and has, to ensure the family will sustain the future. The thought of their disapproval leaves me feeling a little nausea, but I will it to pass.

The closet is full of clothes, all intended to portray a very distinct impression to the family. I slip into them and twirl, surveying the short black skirt, white blouse, and red blazer with four-inch Jimmy Choo signature red-soled heels, eyeing myself in the full-length mirror, and steeling myself for the evening to come. The clothes are flawless, and Chase has arranged someone to come to the house and do my hair and makeup in preparation for the family gathering.

I slip out of my clothes, careful not to wrinkle them, and place them back on the hangers, and slide back into my yoga pants and a long shirt of Chase's before heading downstairs to find him. I sense his presence about one second before his arms wrap around my waist from behind and he kisses my nape. "Miss me?"

"You're so stealth-like!" I say, laughing, spinning so that I can tilt his head down to kiss his lips.

He laughs. "Let's get you into the spa. Sheldon has the room set up so that you can get an entire makeup and hairdo before we get dressed and go and meet your family. Are you ready?"

"As I'll ever be, and the clothes you purchased for me are perfect," I say as he guides me into the elevator and pushes the button for the lower level.

I have just gotten settled when Sheldon walks in. "Kate, I know you liked the way your hair turned out for the last meeting, so I asked Alexis to do your hair and makeup this time, too," Sheldon says.

"Oh, my God. Are you serious? She's amazing! She agreed to come all the way to Italy for me?" I say, sitting straight up in my chair.

"She did, and plans to be here for the next week or so," Sheldon says, grinning.

"You guys are the best! Where is she?" I say.

Sheldon laughs. "She's probably wandering around lost in this palace you humbly call a home. We gave her a suite on the other side of the house. I'll go get her," he says, laughing as he leaves to find her.

"That was very kind of you, Chase. Alexis is amazing," I say, leaning back into the chair.

"All Sheldon's idea," Chase says with a grin.

"Oh, really? I think he likes her. I've never seen him with another girl, he's never even talked about a relationship."

"I don't think he's ever really been the dating type," Chase says.

"Well, he should be. Sheldon's outgoing, caring and such a

great guy. He's got a lot to offer," I say.

Chase doesn't answer, and in a few minutes, I see Alexis pop her head full of bouncy blonde curls through the door with Sheldon right behind her. I scramble to get out of the chair and give her a big hug. "I can't believe you came halfway across the world to do my frikken hair!"

"Sheldon had me at getting to see you again, but then he goes and throws in a trip to Italy! Umm, sold and sold!" Alexis says, laughing.

"Here, sit and get comfy. When we get done, you will be a force to be reckoned with," she says, twirling my hair and positioning me over the sink as she adjusts the water. "I can't believe Sheldon was able to have everything I needed delivered so fast," Alexis says to me as the men talk on the other side of the room.

In less than an hour, she has washed and blow-dried my hair completely straight, a feat on its own, and then has meticulously curled small sections of hair into cascading long sleek auburn curls, letting them fall over my shoulders and against my breasts.

She lightly sprays, then uses her fingers to gently separate the curls before spritzing me again with her magic potion. "There, now for makeup. I think we go for a dramatic image. We can boldly outline your eyes with eyeliner that extends past your eyes, and then let's really play up your lips. They have a gorgeous shape. I'll outline them and then fill them in with a deep red color that just screams Vegas. That's the look Sheldon said you were going for," Alexis says.

I nod in agreement. Something different that will get me out of my shell is exactly what I am looking for to go with my short skirt and black-and-red shoes tonight. "Let's do it," I say.

Her eyes light up with excitement. "Okay, you guys can turn around and see what you think," Alexis says after another twenty minutes.

Chase takes in my makeup and hair, and his eyebrows raise. "You're going to look like a force to be reckoned with once you put your clothes on," he says.

I pretend to pout. "What, you don't think I can convince a crowd of my credibility in leggings and your old Henley," I say, smirking.

Sheldon and Alexis are by the door chatting, and Chase leans down and kisses me on my lips. "I have complete faith that you could convince anyone of anything after your work with Vicenti, but I can't wait to see you in the short skirt and fuck-me heels, especially when they're wrapped around my neck later tonight," Chase says.

"Can't wait to get home. In the meantime, give me thirty minutes and I'm all yours," I say. "Thanks again, Alexis. You did a great job. I don't even look like myself, and thanks to you I am really going to look the part! I couldn't be more pleased."

"Don't take her too far away, I may need help touching up my lipstick," I say to Sheldon.

Alexis laughs. "No, no, Kate. Sheldon was able to get the lipstick we use for actresses and actors. It's not going to smudge or wash off without a special cleansing cream. It's made to stay on through take after take," she says winking at me.

"Seriously," I say, wiping my lips with my finger, amazed that the brilliant red color doesn't wash off in the slightest.

"Smudged lips just will not do! I'm not sure what your meeting is about, but I hope it turns out the way you want it to and wish you the best of luck," Alexis says.

"Thanks, I need all the luck I can get," I say, heading to the elevator that will take me to the second floor of our home. Once in our room, I dress quickly and hurry to return to the group.

"Chase's eyes wash over me, head to toe. "You look incredible, Baby," he says, and I can't wait until we return home and he delivers on the promise in his deep green eyes. We are escorted to the sleek black limo, and the driver has just passed the wrought iron gates and guards that secure the perimeter when Chase pulls me close.

"Your breathing is a little fast. I know you wanted the clothes, jewelry, and makeup to give you a little confidence, but Baby, you really don't need it. It will be you, a Larussio, the only daughter of the most successful Larussio in the family, the only one that has successfully separated and been able to both continue the current family legacy and start a new one at the same time. You should be extremely proud of your father, Katarina. I know my dad is," Chase says, caressing my nape and pulling me closer so that he can kiss my lips.

"When we arrive, you'll go through an archway. It's a well-designed metal and bug detector. You aren't wearing anything that will trigger an alarm and will go through without an issue, but our team has placed bugs strategically throughout the complex. Regardless of where you are, our team will have eyes and ears on you at all times. You have nothing to fear. I'll be with you, and as hard as it is for me, I'll try my best not to interfere. If you need me to intercede for any reason, I want you to have a way to let me know. It can be a look, a word, twirling a glass, whatever you want, but I need you to have a safeword or action that lets me know you want or need assistance or that you're just not able to deal with the bullshit anymore," Chase says, pulling me into his arms and kissing me on top of the head. "What's your safeword or gesture, Katarina?" Chase asks, his eyes searching mine.

"As much as I hate drama, I'm thinking a spilled glass of wine would take the attention off of anything that was happening and give me a chance to react and you to intervene.

"Excellent plan, Baby. You tip a glass, and I'll take it from there," Chase says.

Chapter 27

Chase

Katarina is looking out the window on our way to her great-uncle's estate and then turns to me. "Do you know how much I love you?" she asks, looking up at me with those swirling blue eyes, the ones that have always held me captive.

I fold her into my arms and crush her lips to mine. "I love you, too, and don't want you to worry. Just deliver the message to your family, focus on the Vegas work, and let me deal with the rest of it. Understand?" I say, swallowing back the fear of having her anywhere near someone that wants to hurt her, but knowing that she needs to do this.

She nods her affirmation. The car pulls off the highway, and we embark on a journey down a long, isolated, winding stretch of road into the hilly countryside, where we pass vineyards shadowed by nightfall for as far as the eye can see.

"They all belong to the Larussio family. Your father hasn't been home in a very long time, and he may not have told you how many lucrative and legal revenue streams the family has branched into, thanks to Giovanni," I say.

"He never mentioned that, but in all honesty, I guess I just assumed the Italian family was still just heavily involved in the mafia world, since they weren't interested in Vegas."

"I didn't mean to imply that they weren't, but they've branched out. In all the ways that make the family the family, they are still together. I can't blame our fathers for wanting to distance themselves and ensuring their children never started like they did, but they forget how much of the family's legacy is admirable, ensures that people in our community that can't protect themselves are protected."

"Like the girl in the shop," Katarina says, leaning against me.

"Yes, exactly like that. Innocent women and children that cannot protect themselves against violence. It's when the family steps in, and for that I can't apologize."

"I'll try to keep a more open mind when I talk with them. I've only ever known what my mom told me about my father, his family, and previous life, but I understand that she must see the good in him or she would never have reconciled with him. And I know for damn sure that you would only advocate for helping others," Katarina says, reaching up to kiss me.

"Excellent, keep an open mind, but do not be swayed by your great-uncle's tactics. Just because I believe in some of the causes does not mean I believe in the way he's led his troops or gone about ensuring those objectives are met," I say.

The driver navigates the long circular driveway, pulls to a stop, and the door to the limo opens. I place my hand at the small of her back and guide her toward the large entryway of the Mediterranean mansion in front of us.

As we walk into the grand foyer, her great-uncle greets us with a kiss on each of her cheeks, and gives her a brief hug and extends his hand to me. "I am grateful to you for bringing my grand-niece to our gathering. The family is excited to see her again," he says.

"She's been looking forward to it since meeting with you, as well," I say, guiding Katarina forward with my hand on the small of her back.

"Most everyone has arrived," her great-uncle says, walking us into the great room full of people and servers intermingling amongst the crowd offering drinks and hors d'oeuvres.

A waiter walks toward us, and my uncle takes two glasses of champagne from the tray and extends them to us. "A celebration is in order."

"Perhaps after the meeting," I say, and my jaw locks with annoyance.

Her great-uncle has the good grace to look embarrassed. "Indeed, you are right. It was not my intent to ply my niece with alcohol before she met the family," he says.

"No harm at all. Katarina doesn't usually drink much, but being new to the family, wouldn't have wanted to seem ungracious," I say.

He nods. "Point well taken and understood, Chase. Katarina has met many of the family, but let me introduce you to those she hasn't yet had an opportunity to meet," he says, walking us toward a table of people.

"Many of you had already met Katarina, helped get her mom back when she was abducted by Alfreita. While he's no longer a concern, we still don't know who he was working with, if anyone. We can't be too cautious, as we've learned by the incidents in the last couple weeks. This is why the family meeting was postponed and why you've now been asked to convene on such short notice. I think everyone understands the plan for the Vegas expansion, at least to some degree, but I know that Katarina is eager to share it with you in more detail this evening," her great-uncle says, giving her the floor.

She stands up and starts to speak, and I take a quick glance around the room ensuring my team is in place. "I appreciate the fact, so many of you have come to meet with me today. As most of you know, Carlos, my father, was in a serious automobile accident and placed in a coma as a result. He had a living will created before his injury, and in that document, it asks Giovanni and me to assume control for ensuring that his vision for the Vegas expansion is carried out. This is what I've come to speak to you about tonight."

A few of the uncles shift in their seat, and every fucking one of my security men is on the ready. "While I have no doubt you may have heard about parts of his plan, I would like to share with you what he has proposed, what has already been put into place, and what will occur going forward," Katarina says, earning her a glare from a watchful and intense-looking cousin. I shift a look to him and then back to Sheldon to make sure he picked up on it, and he nods.

"My father has saved well over the years and plans to invest extremely heavily into gambling properties in Las Vegas, Nevada. The property which has been purchased is in the most pristine area of the strip. We have already had four other older properties taken down to make this happen, and I'm proud to say that the footprint of the Larussio is the largest on the strip and will be the most luxurious and extremely lucrative. In fact, the initial return on investments projections is so great that—"

"What about our traditions, what about the money we depend on from the areas your father has held reign over in America?" her cousin bursts out.

"Enough, allow Katarina to finish before she assumes all Italian men are as rude as you," Giovanni says, and I send him a nod at the same time taking in her great-uncle's pursed lips at the exchange.

Katarina continues as though she has not been interrupted. "The projections for return on investment far exceed expectations. In fact, the return on investment after five years will have doubled and is projected to quadruple between the fifth and eighth year. You each have the financial projections in front of you, and what that means regarding income once my father opens. I want you to know that my father has done nothing but think about the family's livelihood, and these numbers are substantially more than you are receiving now."

"You think you can come in here with promises of more money, but that's not what this is about. We make enough money, this is about keeping our traditions, ensuring they live on, and this," her angry cousin says, flinging the document in front of him across the table "is . . . garbage. We don't need your father's money," he says, waving his hands in the air.

My jaw clamps tight, and my body tenses in an attempt to remain calm, and it is with a significant amount of effort that I do not intervene, but she continues as though he hasn't said a word, and I couldn't be more proud of my strong-willed wife.

"I appreciate your candidness but did not come here to promise you money, more to assure you it would not diminish. Carlos Larussio has been heading the family in the States for longer than I have existed and has done it, as far as I have been able to tell, with a significant amount of loyalty to his Italian family. In fact, because of his work in the States, the family's monetary values are off the charts, and the people in the communities they live in are safeguarded. In fact, Chase and I were just talking about this very thing on the way to Italy. There is a woman in a store that Chase and I frequent and saw a week or so ago. The sun was shining in the window at an angle, so I didn't see what

Chase did, but he told me about it. He saw heavy makeup covering purple bruising around the young woman's eye," Katarina says.

The men around the table all shift, or move their chairs, or take a draw off the wine in front of them. One of the uncles starts yelling in Italian, waving his hands wildly in the air.

"English," my great-uncle instructs, and I steady myself, knowing that the Don has put him on warning.

"This behavior is not to be tolerated. This is what I mean. We must not sell our culture, we will not allow innocent women and children to be hurt," the man says.

I watch Katarina let his comment sink in and see the nods from the older men of the room before she continues. "I want to assure you that I am not asking you to give up your way of life, your culture, the safety net of your communities. You see, abuse of a woman is bad enough, but this woman I speak of is with child," Katarina says, and before the hot-blooded heat of the Italians in the room can light up anymore, she puts her hand up in the air.

Once again Giovanni intervenes. "Speak English, or she will not be able to comprehend, and your passion and fight will be for naught," he says before taking a sip of his wine.

"There was a time when I, like my mother, may not have understood what your culture meant, but you know my husband, Chase. He has never forgotten his roots, and there is not a day that goes by that he doesn't live his life with the intent of that culture. The woman I speak of, the one in the shop with the battered face, veiled from those of us that may not be able to see. Chase saw it, and before we were safely in the luxury of his sprawling limo, he made sure that this woman would never be battered again.

"He and my father may not handle things in the way the family started, but cultures evolve, and I can assure you they are quite effective at keeping our community safe and making me and my mother incredibly proud in the process. My father is not trying to wipe out your legacy but have enough legitimate money in the bank to ensure we can safeguard our communities in the way we want. A new day," Katarina says, opening her arms and hands to emphasize the magnitude of what could be done together, fighting passionately for what she believes in, just like a true Italian.

I see a few of the wives touch their husband's hands and the looks that pass between them. I see one husband pull his wife close, kissing her on the temple before whispering something in her ear. "Your father, he gave the impression that he was making a new life for not only him but for our entire family, too. The traditions, customs, the things we hold dear, we do not want to change," one of her other cousins says.

"I do not doubt what you say to be true. My mother was the love of my father's life, still is to this day. Many of you may not know that she married my dad believing that he was a businessman on wall street, with no idea he belonged to the family. She loved Carlos but left after learning he had put a hit out on two people. She never disclosed what she knew, but it scared her, and she ran. And she kept running, changing her name, her looks and doing what she could to ensure her own safety and her unborn child neither she nor my father knew about when she left," Katarina says, and I watch helplessly as tears slide down my wife's beautiful face.

"It was after years had gone by that she learned the people he ordered killed had murdered an innocent woman and were hired to assassinate my mother as a vendetta against my father. So, I understand the passion that you share in wanting to keep your women and children safeguarded. He was doing just that. My mother just didn't know or understand it at the time.

"My father is not trying to wipe out your way of life. He is trying to make sure that our family, in the future, has options, a choice, and that is precisely what I intend to do," Katarina says, but the irate cousin is livid, almost shaking with rage.

"You and your father's vision will not turn us soft. If your plan goes through, the family will go soft. They will be living off the tits of a cow," he yells, but I am no longer watching him or my wife as Giovanni Larussio abruptly comes flying out of his chair, and my security team draws their weapons.

Chapter 28

Katarina

My attention is diverted from my irate cousin when Giovanni leaps from his chair. "Enough! You think ensuring the family's revenue stream is safeguarded makes men in our family soft? I've lived my life outside of the family, building a business, but have never forgotten my roots, no?" Giovanni challenges, facing his family for a moment, oblivious to the fact that Chase's security team has drawn on him.

He looks from the security men to Chase, to me, and then back to the security team who haven't moved an inch. "Holster those weapons. I mean Katarina no harm," Giovanni says, and I see Chase nod to his men, who immediately do, but remain hovering.

"I wasn't comparing how you are living your life and what you've created to what Uncle Carlos is doing in America," his cousin says.

Giovanni's eyes go wide, and his eyebrows raise. "That's exactly what the hell you were doing. There's no difference at all. In fact, it couldn't be more similar. I make my living as an entrepreneur, and you have no idea how. You trust the money I make that goes into the family coffers, but you don't trust me?"

"That's not what I said, or the family means," the menacing cousin says, looking around to garner support from the family.

My great-uncle nods his head toward me and then to Gio. "Your cousin speaks the truth, Giovanni, no ill will meant toward you."

Giovanni towers over the group, looking down at the family sitting around the conference table, before settling on me. "Katarina wants to ensure you and our family can make choices, which is exactly why I branched out and why we will make damn sure that Carlos Larussio's legacy comes true," Giovanni says, handing Chase his business card before walking right out the door.

"I apologize for Giovanni's brashness. He is young, headstrong, and Katarina, while I have never been an advocate of putting money into a gambling place in the States, I can feel your passion about our family, and I feel your loyalty."

Chase guides me out of the room and toward the door where Giovanni is standing. He is about the same height as Chase's six-foot-two-inch frame, but with jet-black hair and dark brown eyes that are brooding and agitated.

Chase extends a hand to him. "I greatly appreciate your intervention on my wife's behalf. I apologize for the security precautions. They couldn't be sure she was safe," Chase says.

"No need for thanks or an apology. As you saw, the majority of our family wants to move forward into the twenty-first century, but my great-uncle and a couple of our cousins would like nothing more than to keep the family in the dark ages and dependent on their past. Katarina, I appreciate you taking the time to come and speak with the family," Gio says.

"It wasn't anything that we weren't expecting, in all honesty, but I was appreciative of your stance," Chase says. "I've been quite impressed with your business acumen. I respect the way you've saved so many little companies, ensuring they don't fold and protecting the employee's financial stability as a result. This is one of the reasons our families are relied upon in our community, along with safeguarding their security. This is the vision that Carlos has, to ensure that we have safe, secure jobs with an ability to watch over our community, so they don't have to pilfer on the streets. I have to say, you've done a great job with your companies. Your financial and operations experience has led to great success."

"Thanks, Chase. Coming from you that's quite the compliment. I'm sorry I was so involved with the European side of the business that I wasn't able to make it to the States for the wedding.

"I understand. The note you sent was shared with me."

"Carlos was the one that encouraged me to branch out. I wouldn't be half as far as I am today without him. Your father is a good man, Katarina, and I'm planning to take a trip to the States to see him soon," Gio says.

"When he is well enough to see people, I think he would love to see you," I say, still feeling the need to safeguard my father.

"I'll send you a message as soon as that's possible," Chase says, pulling me close to him.

"Greatly appreciate that. In fact," Giovanni says, but doesn't get farther than that before Chase cuts him off.

"Sorry, I need to take this call," Chase says right before our security team burst through the front door. "Take cover, get into the safe room, now! Go! Go! Go!" they shout, and all of a sudden I am pushed forward, propelled further into the house and toward the great room.

Gio pushes a button on his cell phone, and the floor-to-ceiling bookshelf spins, opening to a hallway. "I'll close off the entrance. I've sent a text with the password to your phone, Chase. If anyone tries to get into the room without a password, do not let them in.

I'm going back for the rest of the family," Gio says, pushing a button that moves the bookcase and leaves us marching down a hallway while half of our security team lead the way down the hall.

We come to a steel double door and Chase pushes the passcode in, but holds me from entering. "The security team will go in first," he whispers into my ear.

Half of our team have already entered and half of them are behind us. "All clear," we hear, and Chase guides me into the room with two circular sectionals facing each other and two glass-and-chrome coffee tables in the center. The ladies file in with their men, with Gio pulling up the rear.

Gio pulls Chase to the side, but Sheldon stays glued to my side. The men appear to be in a heated exchange with the same two cousins that were giving me trouble earlier. The women sitting on the couch next to me just seem to take the situation in stride, like it's an everyday occurrence.

It's been just over an hour before I see Chase glance at his phone and smile. He looks at me and winks before typing into his phone.

We're clear. Come stand by me.

I excuse myself and join Chase. He slips his arm around my waist, pulling me close as my great-uncle joins our conversation.

"I mean no disrespect, but do you know why people are outside your grounds with rifles, and better yet, why your team didn't see them coming?" Chase says to my great-uncle.

"You have my gravest apologies. Our family can sometimes come under aggression. Chase, Katarina, my men were in almost constant contact with Alfreita's men before your father was injured. We thought we were gaining insight into what they were planning, but my team was fed the wrong information. They believed the hit would take place the following week, that was the second time our security was not good. Your father and I may not see eye to eye on multiple levels, but you can be assured that family will always come first. It saddens my heart to know that your parents were hurt so badly and that our team was not able to intercept. I did not intend to have this conversation with you until we were in private, but you need to understand, I feel a deep sense of remorse that we could not prevent the accident," my great-uncle says.

"Again and with no disrespect, sir, this is now the third time that your security has not been adequate. Recall the attempt on your life and Giovanni's," Chase says.

The older man gives pause and nods his agreement. "Indeed, I don't think the two are related, but perhaps," he says.

"Time will tell. In the meantime, no one gets near our family without the security of Prestian Corp. Jay will keep your teams apprised until we get logistics sorted," Chase says.

"I thought you were the one standing in my father's way, the one that wanted to ensure he wasn't successful and probably, in all honesty, put a hit out on him to stop him," I say to my great-uncle, looking into his deep brown eyes.

"I'm a stubborn man, it's true. I haven't been willing to budge on the Vegas issue, but Carlos is my blood. I would never wish him or your mother harm. I'm a proponent of ensuring the family stays together. We all understand the revenue stream and want to protect our women and children," my great-uncle says, looking at me with nothing but sadness and sincerity.

"I don't understand, then, who is undermining the family?" I say.

"My team thought they had intercepted and got a lock on the communication systems that Alfreita was using."

"Alfreita is dead, it can't be him," I say.

"We believe his comrades are still in business, but I don't have a clue how our security didn't see them coming to our own grounds," my great-uncle says.

"Alfreita's teams have some pretty good intelligence. Once you get a lock on a communication system, they can tell unless you've applied the filters and scrambling before that. They probably realized your team had a lock and then moved to a different wave to communicate. It happens every day, but unfortunately, once they learn you're onto them, they can keep switching frequencies," Sheldon says.

"We're getting the all-clear from our teams outside. They're tailing them to see who they are and trying to get a track on their communications system. In the meantime, everyone is free to go back upstairs," Sheldon says.

"Excellent news. Thanks for running point. Let the men know how much I appreciate their interception tonight," Chase says, guiding me toward the elevator that takes us to the ground floor. As we walk out, we are surrounded by security guards, and the driver has the limo awaiting as we step outside.

When the driver gets us back to the villa, Gaby hugs us as we walk in. "Those boys carted me off to the safe room without a moments notice," Gaby clucks, heading into the kitchen while we follow. "I didn't have a minute to prepare. I usually have a heads-up and can make sure we're well supplied. We don't have near enough stocked down there, Chase Prestian," Gaby says, narrowing her eyes at Chase.

His eyes light up with amusement. "We'll get it sorted, Gaby," Chase says, chuckling.

"If you're hungry, I've left food in the refrigerator, and I'm off to bed," she says, sashaying back into the kitchen.

"I think you're in the doghouse," I whisper to Chase.

His eyes are alight with amusement. "Indeed, it may take one of those super-sized stoves and refrigerators to get a reprieve," Chase says, laughing.

"You know she's only upset because she didn't know where you were. She loves you and was worried," I say, pulling Chase's face down to kiss him on the lips.

"I was making light of it, but I do know that," Chase says, peeking in the refrigerator, pulling out a saran-wrapped dessert, grabbing two small plates from the cupboard, and dishing us both up a piece of silk pie with a cookie crust and chocolate sprinkles. He pushes it toward me, but the events of the day have overtaken my thoughts, and I am not hungry in the least. I swirl the dessert around my plate as he devours his.

"Not hungry, Baby?" Chase asks, giving me a chocolate-tasting kiss.

"Hmm, it's just been an exceptionally long day. I'm so tired, I could fall asleep right on this counter," I say as he takes his last bite, dumps my piece of pie in the garbage, and then places both of our plates in the sink.

"You're wrecked," Chase says, walking over to me and placing his hands under my knees, lifts me, leaving me no choice but to clasp my arms around his neck as he carries me upstairs. The last thing I remember is him telling me to lift my arms, and feeling the soft silky sheets and down comforter cradling my skin as I drift into a deep sleep.

I wake in the morning and flip to find Chase has already left. I slide into my robe, brush my teeth, and head down to find him. The smell of coffee permeates the room, and I wonder if he's purchased some new blend of beans as I pad into the kitchen. "I have cherry crepes made for breakfast," Gaby says, sliding a cup of the coffee toward me.

"They smell delicious," I say, settling onto the bar stool and waking my laptop. "Where's Chase," I ask, scrolling through the media channels while Gaby rummages through the refrigerator until she finds what she's looking for.

"He left early, didn't even eat breakfast. It must have been something important to have him flying out of here like that," Gaby says, bustling about the kitchen.

"Hmm. I know Chase is meeting with the security team and then with my great-uncle around noon," I say, just as the television overhead catches my attention.

Chase is dressed in a black suit, white dress shirt, and my favorite tie, the one that brings out the color of his deep green eyes, and across from him sits a long-legged lady with dark hair that falls in waves around her ample breasts, which are pressing seductively against the wispy low-cut fabric of her dress. She looks familiar, and I try to recall where I've seen her before, and as they talk it finally falls into place. The Italian runway model, one of the many women that Chase used to acquaint himself, the one he was splashed all over the tabloids with.

My eyes don't leave the screen as Gaby brings a plate of crepes with cherry sauce from the kitchen to the counter where I am sitting, placing them in front of me. "Eat, you certainly can't call the dessert you two pie heisters stole last night a decent meal," Gaby says, topping my coffee off.

I vaguely hear Gaby talking, but don't comprehend a word, focusing on the pictures streaming across the top of the monitor. I recognize some from old tabloids, and others I haven't seen. A multitude of images that show them together all over the world, live videos showing her smiling widely, flashing her eyes at him, crossing long limbs with sleek and classic heels. It's her words and the seductiveness in her voice that puts me on edge. "It's true, darling. We'll make an excellent team. I'm so excited about our partnership . . ."

"Katarina, wait," Gaby says, but I don't, barely making it to the first floor bathroom before vomiting, dry heaving and retching until nothing else is left. I am still hugging the porcelain toilet when Gaby gathers my hair from behind.

"Take this, dear," Gaby says, placing a cool washcloth on my forehead. "You don't pay any attention to that nonsense. I don't know what that two-bit hussy's game is, but you better believe that Chase already has her number. He's completely devoted to you," Gaby says before another round of nausea consumes me.

It is almost half an hour later before I am able to pull myself together and make my way up the elevator to our suite, feeling the intense need to shower and wash my overwhelming response to the lady with sights on my husband from my body.

I have just finished drying my hair, and while the bout of nausea has ended, an overwhelming sense of frustration and emotional exhaustion overtake me. I slide under the down covers, intending to rest my eyes briefly, but instead fall into a deep sleep dreaming of Chase surrounded by all the women that he used to date. A myriad of supermodels from across the globe, beautiful half-clad bodies dancing around him, trying to snare him, all trying to capture my husband for nothing more than greed, wealth, and fame, creating a circle that I can't get into.

I don't know what they've done to him or why he can't get back to me, and I try my hardest to penetrate their circle. "Chase, I'm coming. I'll save you," I scream over and over, as loudly as possible so he can hear me over the chanting women around him.

Chapter 29

Chase

I'm just leaving the recording studio when Gaby calls, telling me that Katarina saw the live broadcast and has been sick ever since. "I'm on my way," I say before disconnecting and sliding into the back seat of the waiting limo. I should have known Giselle would be as flirty on camera as she is offstage, but dammit, Katarina should know I have no interest in anyone else but her.

I walk in through the kitchen, and Gaby gives me a withering look and is about to start in, but I'm in no mood. "Where is she?" I say, and she points up the stairs toward our bedroom.

I'm only halfway up the steps before I hear Katarina screaming at the top of her lungs. "Chase, I'm coming. I'll save you! Chase, I'm coming. I'll save you!"

What the fuck! I burst through the door, and she's thrashing in the throes of a nightmare, tangled in the sheets with tears pouring down her beautiful face.

I reach her and pull my wife's trembling frame into my arms. "Baby, wake up. Wake up," I say, shaking her gently until finally her eyes begin to open, trying to focus.

"Gaby called and told me you saw part of the live broadcast. It's not what you think, Katarina," I say, leaning down to kiss her lips lightly.

"I know, Chase. I trust you. I don't know how to explain why it made me so sick. I saw her with you on the internet before. You dated," she says sobbing.

I nod, hating that she's so upset over this but glad that she doesn't think there's anything between us. "It's true, I took her to a few charity events. She's also one of the many women that weren't interested in anything but my money. She found out I was in Italy, contacted me, and asked me to make an appearance with her for the orphanage. Gaby said you didn't watch the entire show. I wish you had, Baby. The orphanage in this area is very near and dear to my heart, and she knows that. She's just using it as a way to get her name in public. I wanted to use it as a way to gain exposure for the children. You know, potentially find people who may be interested in adopting them," I say, pushing her hair away from her face so I can see her eyes.

She nods, and the tears start all over again. "I'm so sorry, I don't know what came over me, some jealous green-eyed psycho took over, and all I could think about was you and that gorgeous woman together. Then I was dreaming. All those women, they were keeping you from me, and I couldn't get to you," Katarina says, wiping her tears with the back of her hands.

I hold back my smile because now my suspicions are confirmed. "Baby, I want no one but you, and it's not your fault that you're so emotional," I tell her, pulling the sheets from her body and sliding the robe she fell asleep in from her body. "Your breasts are changing," I say, circling her nipples with my fingers and tracing the sensitive skin around it. "You haven't been eating well, you've been exhausted, are extremely emotional, and now the morning sickness and wild dreams. You're carrying our child," I say, leaning down to kiss her lips.

"What, wait, no," she says, crinkling her brow in confusion, placing her hands on my shoulders to sit up. "I'm just completely exhausted. So much is happening. I feel like my entire family is falling apart, and then I saw you with that woman, and I just couldn't deal with it."

I smile at her denial and kiss her again gently. "Baby, you're pregnant. There's no other explanation for the changes to your body, your lack of appetite, and run-away emotions," I say, undressing before settling on the bed, grasping her nape, and pulling her closer so I can feel her body alongside mine as I capture her lips with mine.

She pulls away from my kiss. "I'm later than usual, but there's been so much stress. That could explain it," Katarina says, still looking at me with disbelief.

"Three days on the outside of your norm," I say, caressing her breasts and then trailing to her abdomen before shifting her and lifting her atop my cock. "You have no idea how much I love you," I say, easing her down, nice and slow, letting her acclimate to my length and thickness, holding her there, joined as one.

* * *

The next morning, I'm shaving when I hear her start to gag, and before she's even awake I've picked her up and have carried her back to the bathroom. It's almost an hour later before nausea has settled, she's showered, and I've dried her hair.

"I should probably make an appointment to see a physician," Katarina says, smiling at me in the mirror's reflection as I finish brushing her hair out.

"I thought we could have a little fun with the little color stick, first," I say, grinning as I open the lower drawer and pull out a pregnancy test.

"And just when did you decide to get one of those little things?" Katarina says, her blue eyes sparkling with mischievousness.

"The minute I realized you might be carrying our child. You haven't been yourself lately, not eating, tired all the time, and your internal temperature is a little warmer than normal, along with the nipple changes," I say, grinning down at her in the mirror.

"You're so certain, and I'm still processing," Katarina says, chewing her lip.

"I'm completely certain, but this little magic stick will confirm the truth," I say, waving it in the air.

"I wanna see the results. I might just be late, Chase. Stress can do that to a person."

"Indeed it can, so we do it my way. Stand up and undress," I instruct.

"Oh, I like that," she says, warming to the idea, untying the belt of her robe but keeping it folded in front of her.

"Let me see all of you, Katarina," I say, slipping it from her shoulders so the cashmere material slithers down her body and onto the floor.

I spin her with a slight touch of my hand to her shoulder, letting my fingers trail to her breasts while the other circles her nape, pulling her closer as I continue to trace the sensitive and now fully erect nipples, sending goosebumps down the sides of her arms. I lower my hand and run it across her taut belly that will soon be swollen with our child and guide her toward the toilet on the other side of the spacious bathroom.

"Sit and open for me," I instruct and her cheeks color with embarrassment.

"Chase . . ." she says, still unsure of what I'm asking.

"I want this intimacy with you, Katarina," I instruct, opening the package while capturing her blue eyes swirling with emotion. I see the very moment she understands what I'm asking and then watch as she submits, exposing her perfectly pink pussy to me as I kneel in front of her.

She watches with glazed eyes. "Let yourself go, Katarina," I say, rubbing her inner thigh and pressing the wand against her sex as she begins, caressing her delicate skin until her stream has subsided and her face is flushed with arousal. I place the little stick cautiously into its sheath before sealing, cleaning the container, and carefully putting it on the counter.

"We have a five-minute wait," I say, running a damp washcloth through her folds, caressing her, taking my time, rubbing the material over her clit, thoroughly washing her before picking her up and carrying her into the bedroom and laying her down so that I can finish cleaning her with the warmth of my tongue.

She moans with arousal as I find the spots she loves, leisurely licking and sucking, heating her desire with each stroke, building the tidal wave that I know has been slowly growing. Her little belly tenses and I take her clit into my mouth and suck hard, watching her trembling around me, swell after swell while I caress her through her pleasure.

"You are so very beautiful when you come for me, Baby, are you nervous?" I ask, taking her hands so I can hold her against me.

"If you're right, this changes everything, Chase. It means we have a tiny little person dependent on us. I'm so excited I can barely breathe," Katarina says, stroking my lip with the tip of her fingernail.

"Me, too, Baby," I say, kissing her. "Stay here, let me get it," I say, walking into the bathroom. "Green is positive and red is negative," I say before holding it up for us to both see the color of the little dash at the same time.

Neither of us says a word, both caught up in the moment. "It's green. I've thought about this for so long, wondering what it would be like to be pregnant with our child," Katarina says, unable to stem the tide of emotion or stream of tears that flow from her eyes.

I wipe them gently, kissing her delicate lips before removing my clothes to lie down beside the woman I will love forever.

Chapter 30

Katarina

The next morning, Chase lifts me, positioning me over the toilet before nausea overtakes me, wave after wave until I have nothing left to dispel.

A half hour later, once it's passed, he assists me up, concern filling his deep green eyes.

I run my finger over his lips. "I'll be fine, the morning sickness will pass. I just need a shower. When is the lab tech arriving?"

"She should be here within the half hour, but a few things happened last night. We're going to have to meet with your family again later tonight. Apparently your great-uncle has reached a decision and wishes for the entire family to be together when he tells everyone. Your clothes have been laid out to get your blood work, and Alexis is going to do your hair and makeup again for the meeting," Chase says, kissing the top of my head before leaving me to get ready for the day.

Once showered, I slide the skirt arranged on the bed over my hips, pulling the zipper up, grimacing at the snugness, wondering if all of Gaby's meals are to blame or our little one. I rub my belly through the skirt, smiling as I pull the sweater over my head and set out to find him downstairs in the library.

The reading chair has my favorite blanket across its back, and Chase and the lab technician are talking about the test. Chase turns when he sees me. "Katarina, this is Karen. She'll be taking a little blood, and we should have the official results in a day or so," he says.

"Mrs. Prestian, it may be sooner, we've been asked to get this expedited as quickly as possible," Karen says.

"I slide into the reading chair, hanging on to Chase's hand as she wraps the rubber around my arm, slapping my skin to increase the blood flow.

"Mrs. Prestian, you're going to feel a slight prick," Karen says, but I feel nothing except the tightening of Chase's hand on my own. "Okay, Baby?" Chase asks.

I am barely listening to what the lab tech is chatting about, lost in my thoughts until Chase taps my shoulder. "Katarina, Karen was just asking you to release your grip," Chase says.

I nod. "So sorry," I say as the technician finishes up and places a Band-Aid on my arm.

"The results shouldn't take long. Your physician will give you a call when the results are in," Karen says, labeling and placing her tubes in a case before Chase walks her to the door.

"You were a million miles away. Are you doubtful about the results?" Chase says.

I shake my head. "Not anymore. My skirt would barely zip this morning. Seriously, I just wore it two weeks ago and it was fine," I say as we head into the dining room where Gaby has laid out fruit, cheese, and an egg bake.

The plates from our late brunch are just being cleared when Alexis walks into the dining room with Sheldon. "I'm here to get your hair and makeup done before you go to the big meeting," Alexis says, holding up her magic purple bag.

"I know they said no wires or pieces, but I want a mic on Katarina at all times," Chase says to Sheldon.

"The best way to get her through their detectors is to use the bobby pin," Sheldon says, pulling a device that looks just like one from his pocket. This little thing will be able to pick up anything within a hundred feet pretty damn clear."

"Alexis is going to give you a hairstyle that requires a ton of bobby pins. If you do alarm, they'll see that you have a gazillion of these things, too many to be bothered with," Sheldon says.

Alexis shuffles in front of him settling her bag next to the table. "It's called an up-do, Sheldon, now be a love and plug all of my toys in and then shoo," she says, handing him a variety of styling equipment.

Sheldon's lips curl up in amusement. "Always happy to prepare your toys, Alexis," Sheldon says, and the gleam in her violet eyes tells me she doesn't miss the innuendo.

Chase bends down, his eyes alight with amusement. "I think you're in good hands, and I need to take care of a few things," Chase says, kissing me before leaving me with Sheldon in his stead.

* * *

In less than two hours I am entirely transformed. My up-do is business savvy, but sexy, with part of my hair swooped up and held by pins, while the bottom half is left dangling in princess curls that fall down my back and lie against the swell of my breasts in the front.

"Absolutely yes! If you want me to do your makeup before you leave this evening, let me know," Alexis says.

"Excellent idea," I say, heading for the stairs and glancing at the clock. Just enough time to get some work done on The Larussio plans and prepare for tonight before changing. I slide into the clothes that are laid out and spin on the four-inch red platform heels and head back downstairs to Alexis.

In less than twenty minutes, she gives me a hand mirror. "I can't believe how good you make me look," I say, standing and giving her a huge hug of gratitude. "I sincerely hope everything works out between you and Sheldon," I say just before the men walk in to take me to what may be the biggest battle of my life.

Chapter 31

Chase

I watch my wife intently, and it is with great effort that I don't call this evening off and keep her safely locked away in our villa. "You look ready to take on the world this evening," I say, taking in the short skirt, fitted blazer, and bright red platform heels. "Sheldon, do you want to do the honors?" I ask, holding the bobby pin mic out.

"You're really going to let him muss with her hair?" Alexis says, huffing, chewing her lip. I try hard to keep the smile that threatens at bay. Sheldon will have his hands full with this one.

"We can do it together," Sheldon says, placating her. "We need to position the mic toward the front for clarity of everyone in the room, right around this area," Sheldon says, gesturing around the top of Katarina's crown.

"I've got this, give me your little James Bond device," Alexis says, taking it from his outstretched hand. "Will it still pick up if I swirl a bit of hair around it?" she asks.

"Absolutely," Sheldon says, the corners of his lips upturned as he watches Alexis place it into Katarina's hair, lifting a wayward strand around it, securing and hiding it entirely.

"You, Katarina Meilers Larussio Prestian, are ready to take on the world," Alexis says, bowing.

Katarina laughs at her playful dramatics, and I catch the look in Sheldon's eye as he watches Alexis. "I can't thank all of you enough for making this evening possible. I know it takes a team to deal with this type of stuff, and we have the best one anyone could ask for," my wife says.

"We've got the men on the ready, and we need to go. We'll have a final debrief in the car," Sheldon says, taking a few minutes to talk with Alexis before catching up to us as we get to the foyer, exit the complex, and slide into the limo.

We arrive at the Larussio complex and are waved through the gates by an army of burly security guards. They wand us, looking to detect bugs or plants, and as expected, it begins blinking as it passes over Katarina's head. The security guard pulls the one strategically left dangling out of her hair, waves it in front of the detector, and it dings again. "Let her through, hair clips, hundreds of them," the guard says, scowling.

"Sorry, I didn't know there was a dress code," Katarina says.

"It is not to worry, proceed," the burly guard says, and I let out the breath I've been holding.

The dining room can hold at least twenty people around the long rectangular table. Sheldon and our security team are required to stay outside the doors, and once past, Katarina and I are waved to take a seat at the table directly across from Giovanni.

When everyone has arrived, the doors are closed, and Katarina's great-uncle takes a seat at the head of the table.

"We have much to discuss this evening, which is why you have all been asked to attend without security and have been swiped for devices. As you know, Giovanni and I were the targets of a sniper when we flew back into the country, security picked up surveillance at Chase and Katarina's home a few nights ago, and then we were accosted as we gathered as a family. We had no notice that an entire unit with communication drones would be outside of our complex. While intel believes they were merely gaining recon, if they had been planning an attack, we may not be sitting here today. We owe our lives, safety, and well-being to Chase Prestian and his intel team," my great-uncle says, gesturing toward our end of the table. "I know that I have been staunchly opposed to moving in the direction of the casino, but I have asked Katarina here this evening to review the detailed monetary returns. While you saw some of the preliminary projections that Carlos put together, Katarina has been able to package this now with up-to-date construction costs and returns, and I think you will be most interested," he says, gesturing for Katarina to take the floor.

She stands, passing a packet of papers to the person on each end of the table, asking her cousins to pass them around, and when they do, many of the cousins flip ahead. I see their eyes widen at the dollar amounts. Her father is a hell of a businessman, inspired to do something more after her mother left so many years ago. He has saved well, invested over the years, and I know she is proud of him as she spends the next hour going through every fine detail of her father's plan, including the returns that will sustain the family into the future. The Larussio will become the family's legacy. I can sense the acceptance and excitement in the room. She takes a seat beside me, and I take her hand under the table.

"It's no secret that I've been displeased with the thought of moving our livelihood into the world of casinos and have attempted to block this effort at every opportunity. Today, I must sit before you and tell you that I was wrong. The world is changing, and if we are to survive, we must change with it. Carlos started contemplating this years ago when he lost his wife, so he's had time to determine how to move the family forward while maintaining our financial viability. Unlike me, who has continued to live in the present and has not had a wake-up call to catapult me into the future, until now. Carlos Larussio is recovering from the head-on collision with the semi-truck that plowed into his car, meant to kill him and his wife. He saw this coming and set the action in place to protect not only his immediate family but the entire family. Katarina, we welcome you, appreciate you traveling halfway across the world to speak to us on your father's behalf," her great-uncle says.

"Thank you so much for the opportunity," Katarina says, rising from her chair. "It's not clear when my father will recover fully, and until that time, Giovanni and I will be orchestrating his wishes. I understand that while many of you are excited about a new opportunity and what that means for your family and their future, that some of you are uncertain and have grave reservations," she says.

Her great-uncle stands. "I'll speak to this. Katarina has shared the videotape that shows my nephew laying out the course of investments and long-term profits. After seeing that recording, I can be assured that Carlos was of sound body and spirit and had our family's interests at heart. We will be dropping the petition for injunction and the family will be in full support."

"Thank you so much," Katarina says. "While I would love to stay and celebrate, I need to return home and begin work on The Larussio Casino and Resort. I hope that as you discuss amongst yourselves, those of you that are not entirely convinced will come to realize what a fantastic opportunity this is for not only your own future but those of your children and grandchildren."

While all seems fine, my body is tense, waiting for any reaction from the two cousins who have been the most vocal and passionate about their future. They say nothing, which is a concern because Italian men do not sit idly by when they are in opposition to a movement. They either speak passionately about their view or have an entirely different plan altogether.

Chapter 32

Gio

Hearing my great-uncle agree to support the Vegas build is something I never thought I would see in his lifetime. I nod to Chase and Katarina, mulling over the multitude of options and our family's legacy. Uncle Carlos was the one that gave me the idea for a start, the seed money, and continued encouragement to break away from the family and invest in high-class resorts, and now he wants me to oversee operations in America and help his daughter, my cousin, create a new legacy for our family.

I had Katarina all wrong. I thought she wanted to take over the entire family's estate, and she's looking at me like why don't I fucking step up and help her with the task that has been presented to the two of us, and my great-uncle is looking at me the very same way.

Chase Prestian guides his wife out of the conference room. I take a moment to contemplate, looking around at the Italian Family, trying to gauge their mood and hoping to gain some perspective. While I've already made my decision, seeing the nods of approval from the family supportive of Uncle Carlos's dream and vision because of the incredible monetary advantage and my uncle's support is something I never thought I would live to see. It is humbling and gravely satisfying to see my uncle's vision for the future gaining support of the family.

I am preparing to leave and go check on Serena when my two cousins start up again about the collapse of the family. They have been able to play on my great-uncle's concerns before, but he has made his peace, and I will not allow them to continue berating him like this.

"The family has made the decision, and there will be no more conflict surrounding it," I say.

"You aren't in charge yet, Giovanni," my cousin yells.

"Enough. You will show respect. He will be the don, taking my place shortly enough," my great-uncle roars.

I wake the next morning, irritated that I've had to stay in the guest room of my great-uncle's estate while security transported the family and settled them in for the night. After my cousin's outbursts, leaving my great-uncle alone would not have been in anyone's best interests.

I look at the clock. It's barely 6:00 a.m., and I've had less than four hours of sleep, but am restless, knowing Serena is alone except for Antonio and the security team from Prestian Corp. I hit the button that will connect me with him, and when he answers he sounds wide awake and not half asleep as I anticipated.

"Morning, boss. You must have a sixth sense. I was just going to send you a message. We've got a little situation here, nothing we can't handle, but Serena's adamant that she go and see her nonna.

She woke up in the night and couldn't go back to sleep, so she's been baking all damn night," he says.

"She's not supposed to be on her foot yet," I say.

"I told her, but she said it feels fine. I had her sit on the barstool and brought her the stuff she needed. Lucky for me, your housekeeper had everything she needed stocked, or she would have had my ass running around in the middle of the night, trying to pilfer stuff," Antonio says gruffly.

I smile at the thought of the mammoth man running around the city, trying to borrow or steal sugar and flour. "Any luck finding her brothers?" I ask.

"They're all with her nonna already. One of our informants knew the safehouse they were using. It took a bit of explaining, but I had our men drop them at the hospital last night. I thought you might want to take Serena there yourself today," Antonio says.

"Good. I'll be there in about an hour and a half and will take her to the hospital. Just let her know and have her ready," I say.

"Will do, boss."

"Thanks, Antonio," I say, sliding into my pants and pressing Chase Prestian's phone number.

"Chase here," he says, answering after only the second ring.

"Call me on the burner. Jay has the number," I say, disconnecting as I pull my shirt on and step into my shoes before the secure phone even starts to vibrate.

"You know that leak you talked about last night? I think we may have just located it. Unfortunately, he's with Serena. There's no way Antonio could have found her brothers this fast and got them back to the hospital with her nonna unless he already knew where they were."

"Your right-hand man," Chase says.

"It would appear that way," I say.

"We've got men in place with Antonio. Let me give Jay a call. One of us will call you back," Chase says, disconnecting.

I don't know if he thinks I'm just going to sit here twiddling my thumbs while she's in danger. If he does, he's wrong, but I can't go through the usual channels, because right now I have no fucking clue who to trust except the Prestian team who has kept my family and me out of the line of fire multiple times in the past few weeks.

When I get downstairs, my cousin, Salvatore, is in the kitchen preparing a latte. "I need a ride. We may have just found the leak and I can't go through the normal channels."

Salvatore's eyes darken and turn hard. "Let's go, but we need to alert some of the men to safeguard the house," he says.

"We say nothing to anyone but the Prestian Corp team for right now," I say.

He nods as I get on the phone. "Meet me outside," he says as I make sure someone will take care of the family while we are away.

I step outside, and Sal pulls up in a car that I don't recognize. I open the door and slide into the passenger seat. "Your car?"

He smiles at me for a moment. "No, we just swiped the help's car. If you think we have a leak, our vehicles aren't secure," Sal says, pressing his foot down on the gas pedal.

I laugh out loud because at some point I forgot just how badass my cousins really are, but I shouldn't have. The last call is the hardest, and my great-uncle answers, pulled from a deep sleep.

"Giovanni, it's early. What's wrong?" he says.

"We may have a leak in the family. Me and Salvatore are on the way to the city. Antonio is with Serena, and we believe he may be our leak," I say.

"Giovanni!" he bellows, but I'm not listening.

The gangs around Naples have been using our family name to terrorize and extort money from families across the country. Hundreds of innocent women, children, and hard-working men are being threatened with their lives if they don't pay money not owed. Until this, I don't know if I've ever really been proud of the Larussio name, shying away from all it means, but it means protection for the masses, and the thought that it is being used in such a way angers me. "You raised a Larussio, and that's exactly what we're about ready to go be," I say as Salvatore nods his agreement at the heated exchange and puts his foot to the floor.

Chapter 33

Serena

I walk into the kitchen after showering, attempting to use the crutches that were left for me after Giovanni caught me hopping to the bathroom. Antonio is at the barstool, drinking a cup of coffee and scowling at his phone.

"What's the matter?" I ask.

"Nothing to concern yourself with, but we'll need to leave in the next hour or so to make it in time for visiting hours. Our team alerted the front desk at the hospital that we'll be arriving in the next hour to hour and a half. We should at least be on time if they're going to the trouble of getting your nonna ready for a visit," Antonio says, finishing the text he's sending and pocketing the device. He leaves me to my own for awhile and I enjoy my latte and read until it's time to leave. When he walks back into the kitchen, he seems agitated and guides me with haste to the awaiting limo.

He says something to one of the security team that I can't hear before sliding in next to me, slamming the door and buckling his belt as the limo pulls around the circular drive, down the long driveway, and past the scrolled gates that open for the car in front of us and allow our procession to pass. We are driving for less than fifteen minutes when Antonio growls at the driver. "Put your foot down, we've got heat."

We begin passing through the mountainous terrain at an alarming speed, and it's not long before we come to the high-cliff roads, narrow paths, and hairpin turns. I gasp as we swerve around a sharp corner and clutch the seat in front of me. "Antonio, what's happening?" I say as my stomach lurches with the whipping movement of the car that has caused my seatbelt to suck me back into the leather of the car and is keeping me tightly restrained.

"Sit tight," Antonio bellows into his microphone as he watches me glare at him. "Car One: As soon as we round the bend, stay steady but accelerate, we'll bank hard right. Car Two: Make sure they are following you both. We need to get Serena to the safehouse," he says.

We barrel down the narrow path, and multiple cars traveling in the opposite direction and tour buses are making their way on the other side of the narrow passage. No one is passing us, that's for damn sure. As soon as we hit the bend and are out of view of the cars behind us, Antonio bellows out instructions, repeating his previous orders, and our driver banks hard right, guns it, and then banks hard left and barrels into a small clearing with a narrow road. Antonio thunders into the mic. "Tell me they're behind you."

He nods and runs his hands through his hair. "Excellent work! The rest of the team will meet you at the bottom and handle it, just keep the gas on until then," Antonio says.

"We're clear. Let's move," Antonio says to the driver, who seems to have slowed, awaiting the order as we make our way into the hills of the secluded countryside. We then turn and follow a path with vineyards and citrus orchards for as far as the eye can see until a small, modest house comes into view and the driver pulls up in front of it.

"As soon as we're safely inside, I'll give you the word. Get back to the team, they'll need you more than we will," Antonio says as he gets out and comes around to open my door. I unbuckle my seatbelt and scramble to get out, but he doesn't allow it, instead scooping me up and hauling me into the house in his arms.

We've barely closed the door behind us, but I can't take anymore as he sets me on a large sectional couch facing a window with a view of the orchards. "What is going on? Why are we here, and why the hell are people chasing us?" I say as he puts a decorative couch pillow under my ankle.

"Keep your foot elevated and wrap up in this while I turn the heat up. You and your nonna are safe. Right now, that's all I can tell you," Antonio says, tossing me a throw and running a hand through his dark head of hair as he texts out another message on his cell.

"Where's Giovanni? I want to talk to him," I say, but he gives me a withering look and heads into the kitchen, returning a few moments later. "The coffee will be done soon. We need to stay here until I get a few things figured out, but there's nothing to worry about," Antonio says, texting another message on his phone and pacing for a few moments before he heads back into the kitchen.

I pull the throw around me, snuggling into its warmth, still trying to expel the chill from the dampness that seems to have permeated the chalet.

Antonio returns with two large steaming mugs of latte, and I inhale the sweet aroma as he hands it to me. I am just about to take a drink when Antonio's cell buzzes and he reads a message.

He takes the drink from my hand, places it on the coffee table, and scoops me into his arms. "Listen to me, I don't know what's about to go down, but I will protect you. Hang onto me, and I'll get you to the safe room," he says, passing through the living room and entering the kitchen. He pulls open the kitchen pantry, and it swivels. As soon as it does, he carries me down stairs that end in a room with a bed, a dresser, a bookcase filled with books, a refrigerator-freezer in the corner, and a bathroom with a shower and toilet adjacent to it, but not much else.

"Stay here until I come to get you. No noise, nothing, not a peep. If they hear you, they'll come for you," Antonio says as I nod my agreement, and he leaves me to head back upstairs.

It's only moments before I hear a large thud upstairs and men yelling, and I would recognize that voice anywhere. The one I've longed for since he left me to meet with his family. Antonio thinks Giovanni wants to hurt me. In my heart I know that's not the case. He wouldn't have held me so tenderly if he wanted me dead, but I trust Antonio, too. The room upstairs is filled with yelling, and just as I can't take any more I hear boots clomping down the stairs in my direction.

There is nowhere to hide that they won't find me. A safe room is only safe from people that don't have the passcode, and I resign myself to whatever fate may be waiting.

Giovanni walks down the stairs. His eyes hone in on me, but then quickly scour the surroundings.

"Are you by yourself, Serena?" Giovanni says, his dark eyes watchful and wary.

"Antonio was the only one with me, but he went upstairs," I say as Giovanni lifts me into his arms.

"Tesoro, I was worried about you," he says, kissing my lips while pulling my body closer to his own. "I've got you now, he's not going to hurt you," Gio says.

"Wait," I say, squirming. "Antonio wasn't going to hurt me. He was protecting me," I say, and Gio's eyes look sad.

"I'm so sorry, the entire family was fooled," he says.

"Wait! Were you the one following us on the sea road?" I ask, and he looks puzzled.

"No, we followed the tracking we have on all of our security team in case we need to get them out of trouble," Giovanni says.

"Someone was following us, and if we didn't have another driver behind us, they would have driven us off the road. Antonio is the only reason I'm alive and not smashed and broken along some beachfront far below the roadway."

He is contemplative, carrying me upstairs and settling me onto the couch. Antonio is in a chair in the corner, and a tall, muscled, dark-haired man with solemn eyes is glaring at him.

"Serena believes you were keeping her safe and didn't intend to harm her. Sal, he doesn't move until we get to the bottom of it," Gio says, pressing a button on his cell phone.

"This is Gio, I want to know exactly what happened on the road." I hear muffled voices on the line, and he nods every once in a while, but his eyes don't leave Antonio's. "As Antonio has instructed, you will find out before the day is through," Gio says into the phone, and a shiver runs down my spine at the coldness in his voice.

He disconnects, continuing to glare at Antonio. "You have moments to tell me why the fuck you didn't tell me Serena was in danger. You were in charge of keeping her safe, with your life if necessary, and to keep me informed of anything that would have compromised it. Instead, you have her careening around the countryside on narrow roads while someone tails you, almost getting her killed, and I know absolutely nothing!"

Antonio nods, looking at Gio. "It's true, I couldn't trust the wires. I believe that we've got a leak and I didn't want to show our hand. I intentionally kept you in the dark, hoping that our men would get the truth out of our tails, but you got here first," Antonio says.

Giovanni is pacing and runs his hand through his hair. "The same men, our men, the ones with these so-called tails, they could be the leaks!" he bellows.

"They aren't, Giovanni. I tapped them before we left. I've had eyes on them since we left the roadway, and they've done exactly as I've asked. I can show you the camera feed, but I have every confidence the information will be forthcoming fairly shortly."

"How did you know we had a leak?"

"All the incidents lately couldn't be a coincidence. I've been through hours and hours of recordings of the security team and couldn't find anything. Then it started coming together when you asked me to have Serena's brothers found. I gave the order, and in less than an hour they had rounded them up and taken them to the hospital. The only way they could have got to them that fast is if they already knew where they were, which is an entirely different story," Antonio says.

"My patience is growing thin! Leave nothing out," Giovanni orders, staring at him with furious eyes, causing the small hairs on the back of my neck to prickle.

"Your cousin and his crew were already trying to find them and had just gotten word that they may be staying in a safehouse in one of the older neighborhoods. They were getting close to closing in when I put out the order that you wanted them found and there would be a huge bonus.

"Our own blood! Is that what you're telling me, Antonio? They wanted the fucking reward money?" Giovanni bellows.

"I'm sorry, Gio. I wish it were that simple, and I was trying to get the information from the men that were following us. Just to be sure, before I brought this information to your door."

Giovanni doesn't say a word. He doesn't have to. Antonio and everyone else in the room can see that he is about ready to explode.

"I don't know how to tell you everything except to be straightforward. I believe your uncle put a hit out on your parents years ago for the same reason a hit was put out on Carlos and his wife. I haven't gotten all the intel back, but everything is starting to point to your cousin. I think he is the one that put out the hit on your uncle Carlos and his wife."

Giovanni starts to say something, but Antonio raises his hand, while Sal tracks his movement with darkly hooded eyes. "Your cousin also knew about Serena's family's debt, and I heard him ask his crew to find out who would continue payments to the family and to make a house call since Serena and her brothers appeared to be under your protection," Antonio says, clearing his throat.

"Jesus Christ! It was our family all along. This will kill my great-uncle. We deal with it our way. He is never to know about what his brother and nephews have done," Giovanni says, turning away from Antonio and Sal and walking toward me when Antonio's cell begins to ding over and over.

He yells for Giovanni and Sal to get me to the safe room, and Gio scoops me up and carries me to the kitchen and to the door that will lead me downstairs. "Go, Serena, you know the rest of the way. I'll be with you shortly," Gio says, but a crashing sound makes me turn toward it at the same time a vehicle bursts through the walls and crashes into the living room of the cabin.

"Take cover!" Antonio yells as the glass of the window and walls of the cabin splinter and a jeep careens and barrels through the cabin.

"Serena, downstairs," Giovanni yells, but I've seen the driver, and there is no way that I can do as he's asked. Sal throws a gun in the air to Antonio and aims another at my brother who is in the driver's seat.

My oldest brother jumps out of the vehicle, and my other brother opens the passenger side and takes vigilance behind its door with a rifle leveled at the Larussios. "She's going home with us. Serena, these Larussio assholes have been extorting money from you long enough. We know all about it, and it fucking stops now. And you," my brother says, pointing to Antonio, "stay the hell away from our sister. I'm not sure how you got your hooks into her, but she's no longer your girlfriend! She has nothing to do with the likes of you or the Larussio boys you work for. Get in the car, Serena," my brother yells.

Chapter 34

Katarina

Chase and I are eating breakfast two days later and discussing the sudden death of my cousin who Jay and Giovanni's head of security learned was behind my parents' accident. "Everything just happened so fast. I mean, clearly he was against any change from the past, but what makes someone so fanatical?" I ask as Gaby places a pot of coffee in front of us, and I place my hand over my stomach instinctively. "Limiting to one cup. Effects of caffeine on babies aren't really known, and I'd rather not take the chance," I say.

"It's decaffeinated, Baby. I've been having our coffee blended the last week or so. I had the company in Brazil send me some as soon as I began to suspect you might be pregnant," Chase says as my phone rings.

I glance down at an incoming number and accept the local call. "Hello, this is Kate."

"Good morning. This is Dr. Kinders," a warm voice says on the other end.

"Oh, yes. I was hoping to hear from you today," I say as Chase watches me expectantly.

"We have the blood results back from the lab, and first let me officially congratulate you and your husband. You are most definitely going to be parents," she says.

"That's wonderful news, it's positive," I say. Chase's face breaks into a wide grin and Gaby high-fives the air in the background.

"Yes, but there is a little more we need to discuss concerning the pregnancy. Is now a good time?"

I try to control the fear that suddenly overtakes me, already protective of my unborn child. I swallow and try to relax my breathing and am finally able to find my voice. "Sure, now is fine," I say, shrugging my shoulders at the question on Chase's face.

"Your husband asked that we run a full blood work panel when testing for pregnancy, since you've been so fatigued. We found a tremendous amount of human chorionic gonadotropin levels, which is often referred to as hCG in your blood," Dr. Kinders says.

"I don't know what that means," I say as Chase reaches over and takes my hands, which have begun to tremble. His eyes are holding my own, and I take a deep breath.

"While not definitive, it's a typical early indicator that in all likelihood you are carrying multiple babies," Dr. Kinders says.

A wave of relief that our little one is not in danger washes over me, and then the reality of what she said slowly starts to penetrate my brain.

"Are you still there, Mrs. Prestian?" she asks.

"I am. Maybe in a little shock, though. You really think it may be twins?" I say, watching the look of emotion in Chase's eyes go from deep concern to surprise and then to full-blown delight.

"Twins?" he mouths, grinning widely.

"Mrs. Prestian, it's just an early indicator, and we'll definitely need to run more tests to confirm. The levels in your blood lead are extremely high. I don't want to alarm you, but we also can't rule out the possibility of triplets, which is why we need you to come into the office."

"Triplets?" I say, silently amused at the shock on Chase's face, because he usually has well-concealed feelings.

"Oh, dear Lord!" Gaby sputters, a broad smile covering her happy face.

"It's only a possibility, but we need to run tests. I'd like you to come into the office for an examination. Your husband has made me aware of his desire to have any care possible provided at your home, but the first visit and a few others will need to be conducted here. If we gauged your last period correctly, you're about five weeks along, so we should be able to see the babies on ultrasound reasonably soon. In the meantime, I'll send a prescription for prenatal vitamins to the pharmacy electronically, and I'll have our receptionist contact you to schedule an appointment in the office next week."

"Thank you. I'll see you then," I say, disconnecting and looking at Chase, whose grin is a mile wide.

"She needs me to come in next week to have a test to find out how many babies we're going to have," I say, still in a state of shock.

Chase is still holding my hands and squeezes them in his own. "I couldn't be happier, but the possibility never really crossed my mind."

"Congratulations," Gaby says, giving me a large hug. "Chase, I may need a bigger kitchen," she says, grinning widely before bustling out of the room.

Chase pulls me into his arms. "Do you know how much I love you, Baby?" he says, kissing my lips gently, pulling me against his body, our kiss growing deeper before interrupted by a returning Gaby.

"Haven't you done enough already young man? Let the poor woman eat. She has babies to feed," she says, smacking him playfully on the shoulder.

"Good point, Gaby," Chase says, smiling at me and kissing the top of my hair, and as she walks out of the kitchen, he takes my hand. "Come, there's one room in the house that I haven't shown you yet," he says, placing a hand at the small of my back until we reach the door down the hall from ours.

The designer has colored the two walls that are not made of glass in a muted yellow with bits of grey in the mix. There is a mahogany designed baby crib and a matching rocking chair in the room, and it, too, overlooks the sea.

"Chase, what is this?" I say, walking into the room.

"It was clear to me being in Italy and seeing you with a family that it's time we fully embrace our heritage and ensure our children are raised where they can get to know their aunts, uncles, and cousins. I'd like for us to spend more time at the villa. Gio is in charge of operations once things are finished with design, and you can do that from here," Chase says.

"I can't think of a more perfect place to spend time, and I agree with you. We've both been running from a past that was our parents' and not ours. We have an entirely different future ahead, we have different options, and we can still embrace the past without letting it define what we want our future and our children's future to look like," I say, reaching up to pull his face to me for a kiss. "I love you more than words can say, Mr. Prestian."

"And I love you, Mrs. Prestian," Chase says, parting my lips and scooping me into the arms that will always protect me.

Chapter 35

Gio

t first, I think I heard wrong, but no, they're pointing the fucking weapons at Antonio, and he's looking shell-shocked as hell, which gives me the moment of surprise I need.

I draw my Glock, the one I never have to use with an army of security around me. "What the fuck did you say? You couldn't be bothered to find out why your sister barely had money for anything and was working herself into the ground, taking any and every job offered to her. You could have helped your little sister when she was being terrorized and extorted for money. All those years! How could you be so blind?" I thunder, walking toward them, pistol still aimed, looking at one of them and then the other. There's a third brother sitting in the back seat. I don't miss that he's swiveled and now has a weapon pointed straight at my head, but I know that both Sal and Antonio have me covered, and they're not going to start a blood bath until they have their sister. "Serena has been through enough over the years. She is not in any harm, and I won't allow you to take her out of here, because I can't guarantee her safety until we know exactly who was behind the extortion and threats to her life and that of our family," I say.

"You know exactly who it is, it's your family, the Larussios, like it always is, across the entire land! You bastard," her brother yells, waving his hands in the air, and that's all that's needed.

He and his brothers have been focused on their sister, and all of a sudden out of nowhere Jay and a team of men overtake the vehicle her brothers are in, have taken their weapons without one shot fired, and have them restrained.

Serena rushes forward. "Don't kill them, they are my family," she cries out as I capture her into my arms.

"Stop, they won't hurt your brothers," I say, trying to sooth her widened and frightened eyes.

Antonio approaches with her oldest brother in tow, and he swivels under his restraints and yells up at him. "You caused this. You brought all of this onto my family when you started dating my sister. You may not be part of their family, but you are just as bad, the same thing, they are horrible, and you are no better! Pfft!" he says, spitting at Antonio.

I turn my head toward the man that has been with our family for years, and his eyes widen, but he says nothing and instead turns to look in Serena's direction. I don't miss that she looks to him first, then back to her family and then last to me.

"Serena, now would be a good time to tell me and your brothers what's going on," I say as she chews her lip, still looking from one to the other of us. I stroke her cheek. "Serena, does Antonio mean something to you?" I ask.

She looks down for a moment, and then takes a deep breath and looks up at me with those gorgeous wide brown eyes framed in thick natural eyelashes that are now wet with her tears and starts to speak. "Giovanni, Antonio has been nothing but honorable. I, on the other hand, have been deceitful. My family has always been raised to fear the Larussios. When you sent Antonio with me to visit Nonna in the hospital, I didn't want them to know that you were behind it, so I made up the story. The only thing I could think of saying was that I was his girlfriend and that you had my family flown to the hospital in your private jet as a favor to him," Serena says, looking up at me with those sad eyes.

She thinks I'm upset with her, and I do everything in my power to keep my emotions in check because I couldn't be more elated. I nod, stroking her cheek. "I know, Tesoro. I just wanted to hear you tell me," I say, tilting her face up to kiss me, parting her lips, slipping my tongue in to explore her velvety depths and claiming what belongs to me. "I don't know how you've come to mean so much to me so fast. I think I've loved you since you first sassed me," I whisper into Serena's ear.

Her dark eyes fill with tears, and they begin to spill over her beautiful face. "I love you, too. I'm so sorry I thought so bad of you for all of these years," Serena says as I pull her to me, and her tears soak into my shirt.

"Shh, Tesoro, we have forever to right the wrongs of our families," I say, because she is mine, now and always. I hold her warm body tightly, letting her calm, but whoever else is after the Larussios will not be as easy to deal with, and I know the worst is yet to come.

* * *

Download a free copy of my exclusive story, "A Promise" to receive updates, sneak peeks and fun and games through my newsletter.

* * *

Can the love between Giovanni and Serena endure amidst the chaos? And if she continues to succumb to this ruthless crime lord, will she see the danger it creates before it's too late? Read the explosive, enemies to lovers novel, Rise next.

Chapter 36

Thank you

Thank you for reading RULE the first in the Brutal Kings series. Reviews help other readers connect to books they may love. Would you be willing to help your fellow readers learn what you love about Giovanni and Serena? If so, please leave a review.

Acknowledgments

Wayne, my husband, thank you for always believing in me, supporting my passions, and helping me make my impossible dream come true.

My parents and family have been a steady reminder that you can achieve your goals with determination, hard work, and commitment. Thank you!

Karla, my dear friend, who read the first book first and encouraged me to keep going, and who recommended getting other beta readers, because "You can only read a book for the first time once." Thank you for your unconditional support through all the insanity!

A special thank you to all the people who diligently bring all the aspects of these novels together. It takes an army, and I may be a bit biased, but this team is fantastic!

Debbie, my amazing street team, and all the groups, bloggers, and book lovers who spread the word about these stories, thank you!

Via's House of Vixens, is a "private" Facebook group for readers and fans to connect. If you would like to be part of this group, request to join for loads of fun!

* * *

I hope you continue reading RISE find out what happens next!

Untitled

About Via Mari

Contemporary romantic suspense author Via Mari likes to keep her readers on the edge, fanning themselves as the action unfolds and the heat rises. Her books, featuring the most handsome, intense males, exemplify extreme romance, with powerful men who will stop at nothing to protect the women they love.

Via was raised in both the United States and United Kingdom. Since childhood, she has enjoyed reading books that carry you away. In fact, you can still find her in the early hours of the morning, curled up in an overstuffed chair by a crackling wood fire, reading a page-turning novel, especially during the harsh winters of the Midwestern United States.

When not writing, Via spends her days with her husband. She enjoys gardening, shopping at the local farmers market, and walking in town or around a big city. And she loves traveling to research her next novel.

She also loves interacting with her readers, so feel free to connect with her on the following social media sites! If you want to stay updated on the latest releases and claim a copy of an exclusive story, **sign up for her newsletter.**

Made in the USA
Middletown, DE
09 November 2023